Stonewall Against the Center Sea

A Shattered Moon Novel

Joseph Browning

Text Copyright © 2019 by Joseph Browning

Published by Expeditious Retreat Press
Cover by Vivid Covers
Edited by Elizabeth VanZwolle

For information regarding Joseph Browning's novels and to subscribe to his mailing list, see his website at https://www.joseph-browning.com

To follow Joseph on Twitter: https://twitter.com/Joseph_Browning

To follow Joseph on Facebook: https://www.facebook.com/joseph.browning.52

To follow Joseph on MeWee: https://mewe.com/i/josephbrowning

By Joseph Browning

SHATTERED MOON NOVELS: STONEWALL SERIES
Stonewall Against the Rat Men
Stonewall Against the Vulture Men
Stonewall Against Las Vegas
Stonewall Against the Center Sea

Chapter One

Our Story So Far

Everything was fine until Zew, our indestructible barbarian from the wastelands, went and got himself nearly-destructed by being thrown from a five-ton transport vehicle tooling around at forty mph. I know, I know "nearly-destructed" isn't a word, but you have to admit it's better than saying: two linear skull fractures, a fractured C7, a compound-fractured humerus, a fractured femur, and an iliac wing fracture. The latter just has too many fractures to be elegant—a trait it shares with our bedridden barbarian, currently entombed in the high-tech cocoon I'd used to save his life.

The past twenty-four hours has been a horrid mix of elation, fear, adrenaline, and worry. Diana, Zew, and I had left Las Vegas just before lunch and arrived in the Library about eighteen hours later…battered, bruised, and—in Zew's case—torn. In addition to all his broken bones, he'd lost much of his face and skin along the left side of his body, sliding over the rough pavement. I'd regenerated those using the near-magical abilities of the twenty-third-century Panjang Pharmaceuticals medikit I'd obtained by saving Cara, an artificial intelligence, from death-by-reboot at the Las Vegas crematory. I currently carry Cara with me in a metal box it termed a nexus, and we communicate through an old keyboard and Morse code via a single dim green light. It was inefficient but the best we could come up with on short notice given my refusal to carry it in *my* hard drive—aka brain computer.

Oh, and did I mention that Cara infested me with nanobots that are going to turn me into a pile of gray goo if I don't transfer it into a suitable body within a year? It thought it the best way to incentivize my cooperation and make sure I honor my end of the bargain. So I've got that going for me...

The Library is the first place that's felt remotely like 2112, my time before I arrived beneath the shattered moon. They have power, running water—running *heated* water—and access to a real hospital as well as a genuine library. It took me some time to comprehend that the locals used "the Library" to reference several different things. While it is the term applied to the actual library, it is also the name given to the educational campus that houses the book-containing structure, as well as the name of the nation-state ruled by the mad wizard who calls himself the Librarian. It's an etymological matryoshka doll of a term, and quite confusing for the uninitiated. I'm still getting a handle on it myself.

After we'd paid our entrance fees—a book and an eagle for each of us, per week—we entered the Library carrying our invalid friend, whom they immediately whisked away to the hospital. Then they sorted us into dormitories based upon our interests. I was placed in the professional dorms because I answered "yes" when asked if I was an educated sentient, while Diana was sent to the guardian dorms, where everyone who doesn't fit into their collegial hierarchy ends up. We went to our respective rooms, dropped off the stuff we didn't always keep on our person—secured with our own locks, of course—and immediately went to sit with Zew in the hospital until he woke up. He was groggy, but still with us.

Zew's diagnosis is promising, but he's going to need several weeks of healing to get back to fighting trim, and that's cutting it close. We entered with four weeks' worth of books, so he has a goodly amount of time to recover, but we're still riding on the edge: there's a chance he won't be back to normal by the end of that time, and I'm not exactly sure what I'm going to do about it yet. I'll figure something out; worst-case scenario is a ruin run into Denver to look for books.

To complicate matters, the ZZZ Society is supposed arrange a boat to take us to Great Suomi, as part of their payment for knowledge rendered on the death of one of their informants in Las Vegas. However, our ZZZ contact, Allister Brogman, still hasn't contacted us regarding the timing of said transportation. If he sets up the transport before I am able to inform him about Zew's condition, we may have some difficulty on that front as well. I know it's only been a day—one we'd spent almost exclusively at the hospital—but I expect immediate contact from a clandestine society with branches all over North America. What kind of operation were they running, anyway?

Chapter Two

It's the College Life for Me

Now that Zew was conscious, I felt compelled to give Diana and him some privacy, if only so she could yell at him for almost dying. The hospital was located in the educational campus but on the far side from the dorms, meaning I had to walk through the length of the Library before I could get some sleep.

It was heading toward evening, and I took in my surroundings in the late afternoon sun. The Librarian must have designed his compound around the Platonic ideal of a college campus; everywhere you looked, brick—yes, actual brick—buildings stoically loomed among artfully gardened landscapes. Ornately carved benches littered my way back to the dorm. They were made of stained and polished pine, each bearing a brass dedication plaque. Apparently, an engraved bench was the reward in some form of annual competition between collegiate parties, and the winners' names were commemorated and tangibly integrated into the campus.

The area bustled with sentients—each dressed in one of five different colored robes—ambling on concrete pathways that connected building to building. The walkways eventually converged in the middle of the campus, surrounding a massive seven-story building that could only be the library. From the air, I imagined it looked something like a spider sitting in the center of a web. Even though I was exhausted, it took every bit of will I had to pass by the massive building and stay on target. I was inside a functioning educational institution and there was literally nowhere else I'd rather be beneath the shattered moon. If the mountainous building was really full of books, I should be able to work my way through a healthy portion of them in the weeks ahead before I left. Regardless of how long it took me to get back to Deeplac, I'd be arriving with a lot more knowledge about this strange world than I had when I left.

On my stroll, I pondered those random thoughts you have when you haven't slept in nearly two days and are coming down off an adrenaline-fueled road trip. If I'm being honest, I wasn't sure what to expect out of the Library. Although I had many doctorate-level degrees, I never went to college. I never experienced the mindful exchange of ideas, the give and take of academic discourse, or the slow methodical process of knowledge acquisition. All of my degrees were pumped into my head via the jack in the back of my skull. While they were being downloaded, I was lolling about in bed, drugged outta my mind because it increased the efficacy of the transfer. From what I understood, spending a lot of time stoned and in bed was the only collegiate experience I shared with the average student of my time.

The entrance to my dorm in Balfour Hall was a grand double door that opened into a large communal room stuffed with couches, chairs, and tables. A dozen heads popped up when I entered, but all went down once they realized I wasn't someone of note. I approached the hall master behind the counter and asked if I'd any messages. Finding none, I finally sought the solace of my bed a few minutes later.

A chipper voice and a knock on my wooden door woke me at seven the next morning. "Professor Stonewall"—*yeah, that's what they were calling me here*—"we need to meet and discuss your educational options, since you rushed through your onboarding due to your friend's injuries."

"Okay," I called out. "Can you give me a minute?"

"I'll meet you in the cafeteria. I'll be near the *ficus benjamina*."

I quickly dressed and made my way downstairs. After a few inquiries, I found the cafeteria. Next to the large ficus located in the sunny corner of the room stood the brunette knockout who had checked us into the Library. Her garish orange robes did nothing for her, but I don't think there was any clothing that could completely hide her shapely form. She was devoid of any apparent physical mutations, but I doubted she was a sorcerer—I couldn't see the Library using sorcerers for clerical work—so I assumed she had a mental mutation of some sort. I'd already run into telepaths and telekinetics, and I didn't think I'd even seen the tip of the iceberg when it came to all the possible mental mutations. She waved me to a table where she sat and opened up one of the binders she was carrying. I joined her, keeping my back to the wall.

"My name is Eleanor, and I'm here to make sure you're integrated into our system, Professor Stonewall," she began, her voice thick and sweet like honey. "It says that you've a double doctorate in Medicine and Botany? That's an unusual combination."

"I'm an unusual guy," I fired back. She waited for me to finish, her deep brown eyes staring into mine.

"I'm a castaway," I finally admitted to break the tension.

"Ah!" she exclaimed, as if that explained everything. "Where and when were you educated?"

Normally I didn't like revealing information, but there was something in the way she asked that put me at ease. "I was privately educated, finishing my degrees in 2108." She penned the information, her lithe wrist bending supplely with each cursive stroke.

"Is there something in particular you're looking for out of your four weeks in the Library?"

"As a castaway, I'm most interested in the history of the world beneath the shattered moon—"

"We just call it history," she softly corrected.

"Well, yes, I suppose you would," I apologized before continuing, "and I'm also interested in the plants and animals of this place as well."

She nodded and made more notes. "So history, natural history…any other interests?"

"Geography and geo-politics; I'd like to familiarize myself with the current physical and political systems."

"Unfortunately, that information is limited to tenured staff or donors to the Library, Professor Stonewall," she replied apologetically, as if she personally made a mistake and desired my forgiveness.

"That's understandable, I suppose," I quickly responded to allay her apparent distress. "What level of donation are we talking about?"

"Minimum of five thousand eagles, but most of our donations are in the tens of thousands."

"Sadly that's out of my reach"—I frowned—"but thanks for the information."

"The doctors report you have an unusual diagnostic tool you used to check on your friend…" She looked at the papers before continuing, "Zew? Would this be something you'd be interested in selling to the Library? Our offer would be exceptionally generous. I suspect it would be enough to count as a donation, if you'd prefer to arrange it that way."

After a moment of consideration, I responded, "I'm sorry, I'll have to pass on that right now; perhaps after I've insured my friend's health." I was sorely tempted by her offer, but if she was valuing the Nguyen Mobile Diagnostic at that price, I figured it was best to hold on to it—it meant that I'd found something extremely rare. For someone with my abilities, there are always other options for access.

She took my rejection with aplomb and passed me one of her folders. "Within, you'll find the rules and regulations of the Library. We expect you and your servants..." *Oh, how I wish Diana and Zew were present to hear that!* "...to abide by all the rules herein." She handed me her pen and a single sheet of paper. "Please sign to indicate you've received your welcome package."

I quickly read the sheet and signed where indicated, returning it and the pen to her tanned hand. "Is there anything else you'd like, Professor Stonewall?" she asked.

"I suspect my questions will be answered here," I answered, tapping on the binder she'd given me.

She gracefully rose and I instinctively stood as well. "If there is anything you need, please don't hesitate to ask," she replied before gliding out of the cafeteria. I watched until she left and decided to dive into my new collegiate life, starting with a meal.

The cafeteria was buffet-style and composed of various edibles that came with your admission fee. There were others things available a la carte, and I splurged for a cup of coffee and a slice of papaya to go along with my eggs, bacon, and toast. I hadn't seen a papaya in two years, and although it was on the far side of ripe, it was thoroughly delicious and the first thing I ate. I wondered how they were getting them to the Library. There hadn't been any in Las Vegas—at least none that I'd seen—and you could get most anything there.

I opened Eleanor's onboarding packet after finishing my fruit. It started with a map of the campus—both above and below ground—which answered my papaya question; an underground tropical hydroponic greenhouse would allow them to grow locally. The campus was roughly square and composed of just over a hundred acres. It was encircled by a sixty-foot-wide wall of mounded earth that was twenty feet tall and topped with an additional twenty-foot-thick earthen wall encased in a ten-foot-tall double wooden palisade. A small guard station sat atop the palisade every two hundred feet or so.

There were two entrances: the Basilisk Gate and the Chimera Gate. The Basilisk Gate opened to the north, only a few hundred yards south of the ruins of Castle Rock with a large palisaded encampment just outside the city entrance, where the caravans loaded and unloaded. It was through this gate we entered the city before hauling Zew to the hospital. The Chimera Gate opened to a road leading back to I-25 and eventually south to the ruins of Colorado Springs. It, too, had its own fenced enclosure, which—if I had to guess—was another caravan staging ground; I haven't seen it yet, so I didn't know for sure.

A dense grouping of sixty-three buildings huddled within the walls. Most of them were dormitories or barracks for guards, but a significant number were lecture halls, performance halls—I was getting the impression the campus had a strong artistic focus—practice halls, and study halls. At the center of campus, represented on the map by a giant black square, was the massive library, encircled by concrete walkways.

Many of the buildings continued underground and connected with underground-only areas, most of which were agriculture-related. It appeared horticultural—or agriscience studies—was one of the Library's focal scientific disciplines. While it might seem counterintuitive to conduct all their agricultural research underground, it actually made a lot of sense. The climate had less diurnal and seasonal variation, and given enough technology and resources, they could reproduce aboveground conditions with better control over the environment for testing purposes. Nothing was more frustrating to a researcher than uncontrollable confounders.

Something wasn't quite right about the underground map, but I couldn't quite put my finger on it. Sure, orientation maps are rarely precise and instead aim for visual clarity of key places in relation to one another, but when you have a computer in your head, imprecision can be maddening. It struck me as incomplete or incongruous, like there was more going than they were showing.

Next was an area map delineating the borders of the eight Colorado Kingdoms. As this map was supplied by the Library, its territory was placed centrally, hemmed in by four other kingdoms and a large inland freshwater sea. Known as the Central Sea, the water's edge started thirty miles east of the campus. The Library controlled five miles of prized coastland at the end of a large bay, while its northeastern neighbor, the Slave Fields of the Colorado Kingdoms, held sway along the rest of the shore that led to another bay.

The Boneyard was north of the Library but west of the Slave Fields, roughly encompassing all of Denver plus twenty miles to the north and east. To the west of the Library was the Deutschendorfers, described to me by a legless ursine sentient I'd met in Las Vegas as a crazy religious clan of "smoke-happy, alcohol-hating vegetarians" that made you listen to the recordings of the Great Denver every day. To the south, sharing borders with the Library and the Deutschendorfers, was a kingdom I'd never heard of, the Valley of the Silver Lords.

Further south and no longer adjacent to the Library were more kingdoms I knew nothing about: the San Luis Valley Commune, the Steam Lords of Santa Fe, and finally—sticking out like a civilized peninsula in the wastelands—the Lizard Lords of Albuquerque.

I had hoped for more information than just a map and some names, but it was a start. Although it had been less than five minutes since Eleanor had left, I've already resolved that the lock picks I'd acquired but ultimately decided against using in Las Vegas were going to be tested in the Library. I needed information and I wasn't going to sell my equipment to get it.

I started eating breakfast in earnest and flipped from the maps to the text of her binder. The first thing I noted was that the paper was inked and printed via a very old press. The lettering edges were clean, so I guessed a Stanhope press or some such—metal instead of wood type. Given the level and amount of working technology in the Library, I was surprised it wasn't higher-tech, but low-tech always worked and allowed you to use a greater variety of paper sizes, so it was probably the more practical choice.

Like any good sales pitch, the first section was a brief history of the Library. I was surprised to learn that the Library was founded one hundred and fifteen years ago by the Librarian; either the Librarian was a title passed on to successive holders, or it was a single long-lived person. Given that the Librarian was a wizard and the relative scarcity of such sentients under the shattered moon, I leaned toward the latter. Buried in the five-page history was an oblique hint about a large underground complex, re-enforcing that niggling feeling I had about the map. *Well, isn't that interesting.* If there's a high-tech underground bunker or something along that vein, there might be a place for me to drop off Cara and get my "death by grey goo" sentence repealed quicker than I'd thought.

Next was basic procedural information, such as various buildings and services, their hours of operation, and agreed-upon social norms, like noise restrictions. The bulk of the packet was the extended schedule of classes, lectures, and performances. We'd arrived just before the fall quarter and the docket was open to all interests. It concluded with information for those seeking employment.

I closed the binder, bussed my dishes, and headed back to my room. I picked up the medikit and headed to the hospital to visit Zew. On the way there, I noted that the lampposts didn't always match the walkways, a detail I'd missed on the prior trips. This observation coupled with the possibility of hidden underground bunkers triggered my suspicion; I'll need to walk the entire campus and create an accurate map of my own. Perhaps that would give me enough information to put together what's going on.

Chapter Three

Hitting the Books

When I entered the hospital, I found one of the doctors taking care of Zew and asked for an update. She reassured me everything was as expected, and with that good news, I headed toward his room where I passed Eleanor going in the other direction. She was talking to another doctor, but gave me a quick smile as she continued her conversation. I returned the smile but kept walking.

As expected, Diana was inside, slowly feeding Zew a breakfast they shared since he was still encased in the Huang Immobilizer. His left arm was in a cast but otherwise free to move, and once we'd gotten him here, I had cut away additional sections so he could use the toilet. Otherwise, his twenty-third-century cocoon kept him ramrod straight from head to toe. The foot of the bed was about three feet lower than the head, creating just enough of an angle that he could comfortably eat and drink without choking or aspirating.

"Heya Stonewall," Diana greeted me as she placed a bit of egg in his mouth.

"Diana, Zew," I replied, picking up the chart at the end of

the bed. Sure, the doctor said everything was fine, but I always double-check whenever presented the opportunity. Failing to see anything untoward, I returned the chart and sat down in the corner chair.

"Have you gotten anything from the Library staff?" I asked Diana.

"Yeah, someone came by our room early this morning and dropped off some information," she answered before taking a bite for herself.

"If you wouldn't mind, could you bring it with you when you next go back? I'd like to look at it and see the differences between what they're telling you and what they're telling me. Mine had the whiff of a sales brochure, if you know what I mean."

"I do not," she responded, forking more food into Zew's mouth. "I'm not from your time, remember?"

"Ah, yes, sorry 'bout that," I apologized. "It felt like they weren't being entirely honest in the information they presented because they're trying to get me to come work for them."

Diana nodded in comprehension. "I didn't read what she gave me, but I figured if I don't punch or kill anyone, I've got the most important parts down."

"There's also the 'no noise after 9 p.m.' provision, so do try to keep your partying to a reasonable hour."

Zew raised the only arm he could move and let loose with a low-volume, "Woohoo!"

I chuckled. "I'll take that as confirmation that you're feeling as good as the doctors and the chart indicates, but I'll do my due diligence, if you don't mind." I retrieved the Nguyen Diagnostic from the medikit and started a full check.

"What happened out there?" he asked between mouthfuls. "How'd they use firearms in the Lawman's territory?"

I looked up from the flashing tool. "I thought about that last night before I went to sleep, and ran the sounds of the gunfire we faced against a database in my head to see what was attacking us. I found a match—a .50 cal Burinshide autonomous guardian."

"Never heard of it," Diana stated.

"Not surprising. It was a programmable defensive gun that saw most of its action during the Moon War when it was used to guard underground choke points. It could be controlled via a remote or programmed to perform certain tasks when triggered by specific events."

"Like shoot at a caravan passing?" Zew conjectured.

"Exactly. That's the only explanation that makes sense: the Lawman couldn't go after a gunman if there wasn't anyone firing it. If you remember, it didn't do a very good job targeting; it kept strafing us when it would have been more successful concentrating its fire."

Diana's brow furrowed. "Why didn't they wait to attack until the tanker was full of gas—I mean, wait until the caravan was heading *to* Las Vegas instead of away from Las Vegas?"

"That's bugged me as well. I can't figure out why they wouldn't go for the biggest fish in the caravan. Maybe they really liked olive oil," I joked. The Nguyen made a friendly blip, signaling it was finished. "Well, you're still busted up but everything seems to be healing properly, perhaps a bit faster than expected," I announced.

Zew gave a thumbs up with his good hand while Diana persisted on her train of thought, "They must have had a reason. It's not something you'd choose to use on just anything. You'd save it for your best payoff."

I shrugged and ruefully smiled. "I don't think we'll ever know, and I'm not planning on going back to find out." I put the mobile diagnostic back in the medikit. "I'm going to hit the library...unless you need me for anything?"

"We're good here," Diana responded before cleaning the last of the egg off the plate. "I'm going to hang around. The doctor thinks she might be able to remove this cocoon sometime this evening, perhaps even sooner."

I nodded and replied, medikit in tow. "Before you let her start cutting, let me come by this evening and do another diagnostic sweep just to make sure. Plus, my plasma cutter will make quick work of it and spare your ears from all the sawing they'd have to do."

"Will do. However, if you're not back by six and they want to cut this off of him, it's coming off."

"It's itchy as hell," Zew complained.

"I'll make sure to be here before then," I reassured them from the door.

I walked back the same way, hoping to run into Eleanor again, but she wasn't there. I dropped off the medikit in my dorm room and headed toward the library. The giant building had a single entrance—a pair of revolving doors—that led into a small marble-tiled lobby. It was empty except for the two Grynartis 201A police-patrol robots standing guard.

One floated over, scanning me with its laser DNA detection system. "Stop! You are unidentified," it commanded mechanically. I halted immediately. This was one of my pet peeves with police robots: no matter how advanced the technology, the manufacturer always skimped on the voice box when it came to street-patrol models. The high-end private security robots got voice actors, but patrol bots sounded like they just came out of a cheesy sci-fi movie. The snide part of my wanted to mock them: "I am robot. Beep. Boop. Bop." However, I tactfully answered, "I am Professor Stonewall." Their stun guns were nothing to joke about.

The police bot hovered in place with me squarely in its sights, and I hoped its database was up to date. "Name found. Access confirmed. Commencing DNA match…matched. You may proceed. Have a nice day!" It floated back into position near the second robot and resumed its eternal vigilance. I eyed the pair and failed to find any external ports; Cara probably wouldn't mind being in one of those, but getting it in would be difficult. My current plan, if you could call it a plan, was to find some sort of robotic creature that the Librarian had failed to fully protect from hijacking and just take one. If I did it quickly and in the right place, there's a decent chance no one would notice.

A second pair of doors opened into the real lobby. As those doors closed behind me, a floating lamp slid up from my right and attached itself to me. "English, *Español, ελληνικά, Français*?"

"English," I responded, amused. I hadn't seen a Granger follow lamp in a long time; they had a habit of running out of power and crashing to the ground. Try as they could, Granger couldn't figure out what was wrong with them and they eventually canceled the line after a couple of expensive lawsuits—one over a damaged Guttenberg Bible.

It replied to my request in English, its voice the audio equivalent of sunshine and puppies. "I am your lamp; there are many like me, but I am yours. I will follow you and provide light. If you need more or less light, just let me know."

The lobby had marble floors upon which sat several groupings of sentients, animatedly whispering amongst themselves. The south wall was a long information desk, and I smiled when I saw Eleanor standing behind it shuffling papers. I made my approach.

"Hi, Eleanor, I'm surprised to find you here." Not my best line, but anything that starts a conversation works.

"Hello…Professor Stonewall," she greeted me, her elegant chin rolling around the syllables of my name with the grace of a schooner at full sail cutting through high waves. "Would you like me to explain the organization of the library to you?"

"I would like that very much," I replied with a smile.

"The ground level contains administration, public speaking areas, the Juan Matus lecture hall, meeting rooms, and quiet reading rooms. The second level contains the library database and card catalogue as well as the first of the stacks, arranged by letter. The stacks continue to the top floor, floor seven, where you'll also find additional rooms for reading and individual and group study."

"Books are to be placed in the return carriages at the end of each day. They are not to be removed from the library—the guards will ensure your compliance." She pointed to the northwest. "The stairs to access the higher levels are behind you and to the right. Do you require anything else?"

"No, that answered my questions. I hope see you again," I ventured, but she just nodded and returned to shuffling papers. Not the warmest response, but if she regularly worked the reception desk, I'd have more opportunities to talk to her and time to think up more engaging patter.

I found the stairwell and noticed it went down as well as up. I assumed down led to the map vault—which I didn't have permission to enter—as well as other out-of-bounds locations, if my suspicions proved true. I went to the second floor and passed the database room. Within were thirty computer terminals, most of them occupied by a sentient crouched over a keyboard. Past the database room were rows and rows of tall card catalogues—something I'd never seen in person before. Everything was digital in my world, so I couldn't resist stepping back in time. An entire grid of drawers faced me, and I spent a few minutes opening them and pulling out thick, yellowed cards with book and author names, key words, and locations. It was old fashioned, but it made a lot of sense to have a physical data backup under the shattered moon, even when you lived in the Library.

After confirming the location of the indexes, I found the first of the stacks. With my abilities, I didn't need to access either book-finding method. It took me two hours of slowly walking the stacks to build my own database, albeit incomplete—there were a lot of books currently being read that were not on the shelves. The upside was that my index was permanently accessible to me.

All total, there were over eight million volumes housed in the six stories I had access to, and I'd already discovered what looked to be a serious problem without even cracking a spine: based on book titles alone, there seemed to be multiple variations of history. Titles such as *Russia's Nazi Century*, *How Napoleon Won the War*, *The Portuguese Outback*, *Anne Boleyn: Queen Mother*, and my favorite *The Grain Supply of Alexandrian China*, all stood out in my database like proud peacocks in a chicken coop.

Standing in the corner on the seventh floor with my back to the library science stacks, I gazed out of one of the few windows. The campus spread before me like a Cuyp painting, ending at the Basilisk Gate with the caravan encampment outside the walls and a ribbon of highway running directly into the vanishing point.

Chapter Four

Word from On High

Hundreds of books and three hours later, I descended to the ground floor of the library, a sadder but wiser man. My original hypothesis turned out to be true: there were numerous discrete historical studies that fed into this present. Thirty years ago, the author of a book entitled *Systemic Timelines* identified more than three hundred unique timelines that sometimes shared similar events, but each contained uniquely identifiable occurrences. The tome ended with a word from the author, stating she was certain that many more timelines would be discovered with continuing scholarship.

As I read book after book, the little kernel of hope I harbored shriveled and died. I always knew it was highly unlikely to return to my time, but it stood to reason that if I had traveled one direction, it was at least possible that I could go back. But now, I didn't just have to go back, I had to go back on the *right* path; my "hypothetically possible" trip back in time turned into "no way in hell, bub."

I left the stacks a half hour earlier than I had previously intended, giving me a few minutes to chat up Eleanor on the way out. Time was broken, and any information I could have sussed out of the stacks in those thirty minutes would be there in the morning. The world might be unsolvable, but companionship could make it a lot more bearable and I knew where there was a very pretty brunette with a voice like honey and eyes you could get lost in. I came off the last stair into the lobby when a small, involuntary gasp escaped my lips: there were two Eleanors sitting behind the information desk. I momentarily stopped dead in my tracks but recovered quickly, walking up to her...them.

"Hello, Eleanor." They both looked at me. "I didn't know you had a twin."

They answered in unison, "We're not twins, Professor Stonewall, we are Eleanor-model anticipadroids. There are thirty-six of us on campus." One of them reached beneath the counter and produced a bottle of whiskey and a glass. She poured a double and indicated it was for me. "We anticipate you would like one of these. It's not uncommon for misunderstandings to occur with new professors."

I downed the proffered drink, shaking my head at the fact that my thoughts were common enough that they had a bottle of hooch behind the library desk for all the schmoes like me. Nothing like finding out the lady you're interested in is a robot, a real cherry on top of today's disappointment sundae.

"If you would like to know about anticipadroids, please reference volumes TJ211.14367 through TJ211.14375.

They're on the sixth floor."

"I'll do that. Thanks for the drink."

"You're welcome. If there is anything you need, please don't hesitate to ask."

I climbed the stairs and found the proper section. After ten minutes of scanning period-appropriate literature, I got the gist. Anticipadroids were very advanced, semi-aware cybernetic organisms that took the form of beautiful males or females. They were programmed to anticipate the desires of their owners and others they were directed to please. No wonder I found Eleanor attractive—she was literally made that way. I felt slightly less embarrassed but thankful that Diana and Zew didn't know—I'd never hear the end of it!

I'd have to rush to make my appointment with Zew, but I wanted to peruse the only contemporary reference regarding anticipadroids before I left for the hospital. An additional five minutes of skimming revealed that most of those that remained below the shattered moon were prone to malfunction, especially those found in the wild. The author speculated that the "controlling signal" that once kept them focused and on task had ceased to transmit, resulting in many strange behaviors. Apparently, such anticipadroids would "adopt" a single creature and serve them faithfully. It wasn't uncommon to find an anticipadroid cutting down trees for a family of beavers, catching mice for an owl with chicks, or raising soybeans for food for a school of fish. Most of the time, the anticipadroid ended up eventually killing what it adopted via too much care, but when such a thing happened, it simply moved on to another creature to care for.

Well, well, well…commonly malfunctioning robots, you say? Sounds like the perfect place to drop and hide Cara. It could take over one of the bodies and once outside of the Library; any peculiar behavior on its part would be par for the course.

I made a resolution to return tomorrow and read everything the library had about anticipadroids; I needed to understand their technical schematics and learn their vulnerabilities. Hopefully, they had a jacking system I could use to get Cara in, otherwise I had to find a tinker willing to incur the ire of the Librarian, a path I would prefer to avoid but one that might be worth the risk.

And there were Cara's wishes to consider. As a sentient program, I was still philosophically grappling with whether Cara had feelings per se, but I knew I couldn't force it somewhere and expect it to call off the nanobot infestation crawling over my skin afterward. I needed it to be satisfied with the situation to lift my death sentence.

I hurried to my dorm room, picked up the medikit, and hustled to the hospital, arriving a few minutes before six. "Did the doc give the okay on removing the Huang Immobilizer?" I immediately asked upon entrance.

"Yep," Zew responded. "You took your time."

"I got held up at the library and found out a lot today," I explained. "Let me scan you again and then get you out of there." When the diagnostics confirmed the doctor's assessment, I pulled out the plasma cutter and got to work. Diana helped me balance the large bulky pieces, and soon we were left with pile of them and a mobile Zew.

I removed the last section and pronounced, "You are now free to move about the cabin," before I realized they wouldn't get the joke. "I'm sure they've told you to take it easy, right? No lifting anything heavier than ten pounds, no quick movements, etc., etc..."

Zew nodded, vigorously scratching, "Glad to be out of that thing."

"All right, what did you find out?" Diana inquired. I shared my discovery about time beneath the shattered moon, which elicited a laugh from Diana. "It would explain why all the castaways say so many different things. Surprised it took you this long to put it together."

"I figured something was off, but, you know, I had kinda hoped I could one day go back."

"Living in hope is a terrible thing, Stonewall. Sentients in control of their destiny need no hope. Hope is for the powerless."

"Agreed," chimed in Zew. "The strong have passion; the weak have hope."

Most depressing fortune cookies ever, I thought to myself. "All right, all right…advice received."

"How long do you think he should stay in here?" Diana changed the subject.

"That's up to the doctor, but I don't think very much longer. He can move about now and as long as he doesn't do anything stupid, he should be fine."

"He's not going to do anything stupid." There was a finality in her tone—it was both a statement and an order. "Any word from the contact?"

"Still nothing. I'm surprised, but it should happen in a few days. If it doesn't, we'll just assume it's not going down and secure our own transport. You need anything before I go back to my room?"

"Naw, we're good," Diana answered while scratching the spot in the middle of Zew's back that he couldn't reach.

I returned to Balfour Hall, and my entrance attracted the attention of a waiting sentient. His blotchy skin contained at least four different shades of red and green. He wore the black robe favored by the older sentients I'd passed on campus; I assumed they were tenured staff, but hadn't asked to verify.

"I'm Allister Brogman," he introduced himself, putting forth a six-fingered hand. "I'd like to speak to you in private."

I returned the handshake. His hands were callused and hardened, not what I'd have expected from an academic. "Let's take one of the benches outside." He agreed and we exited, plopping down on the nearest bench.

"Emily's informed me that I'm to provide transport from the Slave States of Colorado to Greater Suomi for you and two other travelers," he spoke once we'd settled ourselves and made sure no one could overhear. His voice was quiet but not conspiratorial; he obviously had experience in being covert while not appearing as such.

"That's correct, but we've run into a snag. One of us has been seriously injured and is in the hospital, although he may be out in a day or two."

"How seriously? I've already booked passage on the *Dianago* a week from now."

"I don't think we can manage travel in a week's time. He's really beat up—barely made it past the Red Line Raiders— and he needs to heal in an environment that doesn't involve pounding away in the hull of ship. Any way to reschedule?"

"It's possible, but trade thins out toward winter on the northern part of the Center Sea, so it's not going to be easy. Not a lot of boats heading north into winter."

"We'd really appreciate it. My apologies for the hassle."

He stood and shook my hand again, "I'll contact you in a few days with a new schedule. I'll try to find the latest ship I can."

I put on airs of returning to Balfour but instead tailed Brogman to find out where he went after talking with me. I was still upset that I hadn't had the chance to infiltrate the ZZZ in Las Vegas and hoped their agent here would be an easy mark. He ended up at the library, but that didn't really tell me much and I didn't want to follow him inside—that would probably be obvious, if he was paying any attention. And you know what? I'd had so many disappointments today that this last one didn't even bother me.

I dropped by the hospital to let Diana and Zew know Brogman made contact and learned that Zew would be released the next morning. They both looked pleased at his eminent discharge; even when you know everything's going to be fine, time spent in a hospital is draining. I imagined it would be doubly so for those two, considering they had no experience with hospitals and rarely got hurt to begin with.

Chapter Five

A Voice in My Head

I woke up the next day to a happy surprise: a recorded message from my bug.

Stonewall, this is Elissa again. I guess there's no way for you to communicate back or else you would have responded already. I realized you may be wondering how you're getting this message when so far away—I had to ramp up your bug in order to fix it, so it's got an extremely long range now. If I calculated everything correctly, you should be able to hear it from just about anywhere, except for the other side of the planet. I'm going to put the bug in your room, but I thought I should give you an update on what's going on first.

*As you already know, we've been searching through the ruins of the Lancaster Building, and it's turned out to be a real treasure trove. It looks like the crazy vultures weren't using or passing along much of what they took from us, so we've managed to get back years of tribute. And there wasn't just ours—there was **years** of tribute from* *neighboring settlements, too.*

Abigail decided to give a considerable amount of their loot back to them, and with the vulture men gone, they have decided to join forces with us under her leadership. The new nation is called Absylvania—which Abigail was dead-set against, but we won the vote and the name stays. I think such attention and displays of devotion make her uncomfortable, but she'll have to learn to live with it. Sound familiar?

Even from hundreds of miles away, she still found a way to tease me. That's Elissa, irrepressible.

So far, the communities have agreed to set up an inter-settlement council, so each has a voice in how larger decisions will impact their locality but the whys and wherefores have yet to be decided. At least, that is the situation as explained to me by Marilyn—I'm not a council member yet.

Oh, Marilyn's pregnant! She's not very far along, but she's already started getting me ready to do the heavy lifting once she gets closer to birth. She doesn't know how many she's having, but she knows she's not going to have as much time as she used to when the little ones come. So I have my work cut out for me in the near future.

Erm, what else has happened...? Oh yeah, one of the

mushroom people that you'd mentioned showed up on our doorstep a few days after you three disappeared and asked if Deeplac and the Mushroom People could be friends, so we've got a brand new group to trade with. Which is great for Deeplac but bad news for you—they grow tastier mushrooms than you did...do.

I hope you're getting this, Stonewall. I'm looking forward to seeing you again. Efte says 'Hi,' and wants me to tell you that it was Dr. Bouchard who was being naughty, whatever that means.

Bouchard, eh? He was my twenty-second kill when I worked for The Company—a thoroughly unpleasant drug smuggler with a sideline of experimenting on slave children. Not that The Company cared about that, but they did care that they weren't getting their cut. Well then, he'll be the first in line if Efte ever needs another shadow person of mine to make an item; it'd serve him right.

Since this was only the second recording I'd received from her, she must have placed the bug in some sort of signal-inhibiting storage container; otherwise, I would have continuous audio like I did before. I'm certain Marilyn has a few of those hanging around or could whip one up in a pinch. I wish Elissa had placed the bug somewhere I could listen in on gossip, but she's far too considerate of others to do that.

After my morning exercises but before breakfast, I made a

trip to the bursar to exchange another House Flores note for coins. They didn't bat an eye and I walked out with another sixty eagles, leaving me with a single note of the same value. I could have changed it, but I was already lugging around so much gold and silver, I felt a little like a bullion dealer. At least the coins' weight was easy to distribute.

Since I was flush, I splurged for more coffee and papaya and enjoyed a languid breakfast before taking my first real dive into the library. Yesterday was a targeted skim into the history section and anticipadroids, today would be a deep dive into both. The two Grynartis 201A robots didn't even acknowledge my presence today, and I reflexively nodded at one of the Eleanor-model anticipadroids at the information desk, even though there wasn't any reason to—it's not like I could hurt its feelings by ignoring it.

I stopped at the database room and claimed one of the computers after a brief wait in line. It was a very basic affair, allowing you to search by subject, title, or author, but it did have a handy jack labeled "For Approved Use Only" so there was some potential there were I ever so inclined. I assumed they'd have protection against illegal jacks, but the 'ware I have was the crème de la crème of my time, and these boxes were generations older than that. After my cursory examination, I closed down my searches and surrendered the station to a waiting sentient.

I first hit the anticipadroid section. It took me until lunch, but I finished every volume they had. Originally conceived in Japan, where robotics was generally more accepted because of their population-aging crisis, anticipadroids were used as servants and companions before gaining traction worldwide. They were programmed to anticipate the desires and needs of their clients by collecting and processing biometric data, visual and verbal cues, and body language. In short, they knew what you wanted before you even knew. With a skeleton of carbon nanotubes covered in flesh, different skins and cultural templates could be applied per client preference, and the higher-end models could do basic feature modifications. Having learned the history, I felt significantly better for my attraction to Eleanor; a beautiful woman that seems to know exactly what I want all the time—what moron wouldn't fall for that? She even picked a table and seat where I could keep my back to the wall when we first met.

In even better news, I was certain I'd be able to hack into one of them and provide a body for Cara. Now I just needed to convince Cara it was a good idea and devise a plan to isolate and incapacitate an Eleanor. Thankfully, the books made the latter much easier than it could have been—I enjoyed the irony of the Library providing me the blueprints on how to hijack one of their own robots. I grabbed lunch, returned to my dorm, and pulled out the nexus and keyboard to communicate with Cara.

"Cara, this is Stonewall," I typed.

"About time. I take it you've been busy," it flashed back in Morse code.

"Yeah…things were hectic, but we made it. I'm in the Library now and I think I've hunted down a possible body for you, but I wanted to make sure it was doable—didn't want to get your hopes up without something solid. That's why it took me so long."

"I take it you found something."

"Are you familiar with anticipadroids?"

"I have a passing knowledge. Eduardo spoke about saving up enough to purchase a defective one that he could repair. From his conversation, I understand the basics."

"Well then, you'll be glad to know there are thirty-six of them in the Library, and seeing as they're known for malfunctioning, I figured putting you into one of them would be just about perfect."

"It's unlikely that the Librarian's anticipadroids would be prone to malfunction; from what I gathered from Eduardo, the Librarian is a remarkable tinker. While I have no objection to the form, I'm not sure it's a good idea. I suspect I'd be hard pressed to make a clean escape."

"What if you had a distraction of some sort? Could you take over an anticipadroid and continue to function as one until I could figure out a distraction?" I typed.

"It would need to be a significant distraction and it would need to be soon. I'm not going to live as a slave."

"I understand. Alternatively, there's a jack into the mainframe at the library computer stations that would take the nexus."

"That wouldn't be much of a solution. I'd have to hope a mobile platform would eventually interface with the system that I could jump into. I'd place that option as less desirable than an anticipadroid."

"Okay, so it sounds like we have a possible plan with a few contingencies. Which would you prefer: waiting to hijack until after I've come up with a distraction or before?" For the first time, there was a noticeable delay in its generally rapid-fire response time. For the first time since I had known Cara, it actually had to *think* about something. It was interesting to contemplate—a silicone consciousness making a hard decision.

"I would prefer to inhabit the body before the plan is completely fleshed out."

I figured that would be its preference and why I presented my findings the way I had. If Cara had a body, at least it would be free of me, regardless of what happened afterward. I typed back, "And I would prefer to be free of the nanobots. How exactly are you going to remove them?"

"Once I'm in a body that can vocalize, I have a deactivation phrase that will end their programming."

Clever. "All right then, I'm signing off. I'll get working on snagging a body for you. If things go as planned, it shouldn't be more than a day or two."

I put away the keyboard and nexus and trekked over to Ali Hall, the guardian dorm that housed Diana and now Zew. I knocked on their door and Diana let me in. I told them the nuts and bolts of Elissa's message, keeping the more personal jabs to myself, and both of them were excited to hear from home. Now that Zew was out of hospital, neither of them were pleased that I had asked Brogman for a later ship, but I insisted. I'm a doctor and they're not, so as far as I was concerned, they didn't have any say in the matter—I wasn't going to risk an on-board injury that could be avoided by simply staying put for a few more weeks.

Before I left, I remembered Diana's onboarding packet. "Diana, do you think I could look at the packet the Library gave you?" She dug it out of one of the drawers and handed it to me. "Do you mind if I keep it?"

"It's all yours. If we need another, Zew's got one."

I nodded and made my exit—it time to find a tinker who was willing to make a very particular piece of equipment for me. One of the underground bunkers was tinker territory, and my status as Professor gave me access, at least to their common room. *Someone's gotta be hard up for some eagles.*

Chapter Six

The Right Tool

On my way to the bunker, I encountered a small building surrounded by gravel that wasn't on any of the maps. It wasn't much larger than a shed, but a concrete path led to it and I followed, curious as to what it was. A small metal plaque was attached to the center of the solid wooden door that was the only entrance. It read: "Sorcerers Only."

I rarely allowed a sign to dictate my behavior, so I opened the door. An intricately carved marble spiral staircase filled the entire inside, illuminated by a single flickering torch. I heard footsteps coming up the stairs, so I quickly closed the door and hid behind the shed itself. The door opened and footsteps crunched along the gravel directly toward my hiding spot. Having nothing else to hide behind and nowhere else to take cover, I silently dropped to ground, leaned against the shed, and pretended to be napping.

The footsteps stopped and a voice rasped, "It is best to obey the signs."

I opened my eyes, fully intending to lie to the guard until I saw the body attached to the voice: an animated skeleton, eyes filled with flames, and a sword and shield in hand.

"Um...okay. I'm sorry." There are times in life when a little white lie to save your butt wouldn't do any harm, but this didn't seem like one of them.

"Don't do it again," it growled before returning inside.

I shakily got to my feet and marked that building off my exploration list as I continued to the tinkers' bunker complex. I could deal with sentients, robots, and with enough time and preparation, security systems, but I drew the line at animated skeletons. Magic gave me the heebie-jeebies, because it just didn't have any limits—or to be more precise, I didn't know what limits it had and there wasn't any real way for me to find out. While I prided myself on being an open-minded twenty-second-century guy caught under the shattered moon, when it came to anything sorcerous, I avoided it like the mighty-thewed barbarians of literature. However, I did label the structure "Entrance to the Sorcerers' Library" based on the signage, the remarkable number of human-looking sentients visiting the shed whenever I passed it again, and of course, the animated talking skeleton.

After that unnerving encounter, the tinkers' bunker was blessedly mundane. It had a similar aboveground entrance and staircase leading down, but this one was illuminated by a good old-fashioned incandescent lamp. The stairs debouched into a large marble-floored lobby with an information desk staffed by an Eleanor at one end. I walked past the furniture and lounging tinkers to the desk.

"Hi Eleanor," I said with a smile. "I'd like to inquire about hiring a tinker to make an object for me."

"Professor...Stonewall, nice to see you again!" she responded with such genuine pleasure that if I didn't know better, I'd swear she was flirting with me. "If you would put your name on this list, along with a brief description of what you desire and an offered price, it will be instantly updated to all the onsite tinkers," she instructed as she handed over a tablet computer. Unsurprisingly, the tinkers had all the good tech.

The system in place was designed to streamline and standardize requests for the ease of the tinkers, so unfortunately there was no way for me to access the entire list to get a better handle on an appropriate offer. I entered my information and took a stab at a price: four eagles. That's a month's "rent" at the Library, a tidy sum for what I needed. The device wasn't that complex, it wouldn't need to work forever, nor would it require any rare or unusual materials like the klarklon that my M1B used. It was, however, particular and precise—it took me ten minutes to get the specs down for the object requested. As I returned the tablet to Eleanor, it emitted a beep.

She looked down and released another of those devastating smiles. "Looks like your offer's already been accepted! Professor Paraskevi will be here shortly; please take a seat." Her elegant arm fluidly waved toward a row of red leather seats next to the keypad-protected door that led further into the complex. "If there is anything you need, please don't hesitate to ask."

Five minutes later, an octopoid sentient exited the secure door and greeted me, "You are Professor Stonewall?" From the name, I guessed the tinker was female, but there were no outward signs as such, not that I would know how to sex an octopus even if there were. She was just over four feet tall and spoke her "Ps" and "Fs" as if they were "SHs," but was easily understandable. She carried a tablet like the one the Eleanor had handed me.

I stood and nodded. We shook hand to tentacle. "I'm Professor Paraskevi. I will build the object you desire. Please follow me." She turned, holding the door open for me. We walked down a long and wide hall before entering her private workspace. She offered me a seat and took her own behind her desk.

"This thing you want me to build, it only flashes lights in a particular pattern?"

I nodded. "That's all it needs to do, but the lights must be at the precise wavelength and frequency, and the timing between the flashes must be equally precise."

"It's an odd request."

"I'm a castaway, and it's something I lost from other time that I would like to have again. My mother gave it to me when I was rather young," I explained. In my experience, the castaway angle just about validated any strange request or behavior to the shattered moon natives, who generally believed castaways were only a few steps away from nuts.

Her knobby head nodded floppily. She was adapted for land-living but still appeared to be mostly—if not completely—boneless. "You put that you'd like it as soon as possible."

"Yes. I don't know when I'm going to have to leave, but anytime during the next few days should serve nicely."

"None of this seems to pose a problem. I should be able to make this for you in a few minutes. You have the eagles with you?"

I took them out of my belt and put them on her desk.

"Excellent!" she replied, rubbing four of her tentacles together. She scooped up the coins with one arm, depositing them in a safe behind her desk that I could hear but couldn't see. Once payment was secured, multiple arms shot out in various directions, pulling bits and pieces from different drawers. She bounced between four cabinets with clear drawers that contained hundreds of different electrical bits and bobs, placing them all atop her worktable.

I waited in silence as she climbed atop the table and rapidly assembled the various pieces she'd just acquired. It took less than three minutes to put together a tube the size of an old laser pointer with a small sliver sticking out from the end. Once the pieces were assembled, she dropped some gray goo on the item, grabbed a small battery, and powered it up.

Once on, the colored LED lights on the protruding end lit up, and the sliver folded down and quickly spun, creating a miniature light show from just that one piece in motion. The only problem was that the colors and timing were not to spec. I was about to voice my concern when she qualified, "I'll program the correct sequence in a second. Please confirm what I've provided is an accurate approximation of your request and double-check the light sequence before I lock it in." One of her arms pointed to the tablet on her table.

I nodded at the general gist of the tube and picked up the tablet, verifying the information while she moved back to her desk and plugged in one end of the new device into her tablet. She then activated the device again and, as far as I could tell, it worked perfectly.

"Looks perfect!" I exclaimed, putting a little warble in my throat to sell my story. "Just like I remember it."

"It's all yours then, Professor Stonewall. Please don't hesitate to ask if there's anything else you need," she replied, echoing the Eleanors' goodbye. She escorted me out of the locked area and I immediately approached Eleanor to put forth another request, after ensuring I could exclude Professor Paraskevi as a potential respondent. This second request was to verify that the device she'd made for me was precisely to spec—I couldn't risk being even the tiniest bit off if I wanted a successful anticipadroid capture. I put an eagle up for offer and again, it was taken immediately, this time by Professor Ilesanmi.

Ilesanmi was a near human who, when informed of my faux-reason for wanting an accurate reproduction of a childhood item, told me he was also a castaway. This was the first time I'd heard of a castaway becoming a tinker and dug into his past a bit as he put my new device through a series of scanners. He'd stumbled upon some nanites when processing scavenged items and they infested him. Instead of turning into a pile of goo as many do, he survived by learning to control his uninvited guests. If only there was a way to ask about such a process without informing him of the particulars of my unfortunate nanobot infestation.

After a battery of tests lasting nearly an hour, Ilesanmi confirmed the device was to specifications. I returned to my dorm room to deposit my new "toy" and settled in with Diana's welcome packet. It was a close duplicate of mine, except that it contained an entertainment section. Apparently, professors don't need amusement; they have reference stacks. In the audio/visual building adjacent to the library, they showed four to six hours of old TV or movies daily. I recognized a little over half of the titles listed on the schedule and figured the rest were probably associated with different timelines than my own.

It was hard to imagine how difficult it had been to put together that there were multiple pasts. In my own time, anything pre-industrial was difficult to decipher, and we only had a single timeline to deal with. Say what you will about mad wizards, it was a monumental achievement and a testament to the quality of the Library's scholarship.

Also nestled under "entertainment" was the battle

chamber, a virtual reality area where one could battle a series of holographic entities at differing difficulty levels. There were eight holopods in total, allowing up to eight contestants to battle each other or engage in individualized combats against computer-generated opponents. This was technology far beyond what I was familiar with; Diana would want to know about it and Zew, too, but I think both Diana and I would place simulated combat squarely under the header of "something stupid" for our recovering warrior. This was definitely a packet for guardians; just thinking of a robed academic like Allister Brogman in holographic combat made me chuckle as I put the packet away and headed to the library.

I had several hours until dinner and even though I can go through about a page per second, it would still take an incredible amount of time to just scratch the surface of all the knowledge held in the stacks. I'd decided that since history was all donked up, I should focus on books about the timeline and reality I'm living in now. There were enough creatures, magic, spirits, technology, and mutations—or abilities, as the natives term them—to occupy my time.

I managed to get through nearly fifty books before I needed some food, and dinner brought a pleasant surprise: Brogman. He was waiting in the cafeteria when I entered. I got some food and sat down at his table.

"I've wrangled another ship for you. It leaves on the twenty-fifth, if that's acceptable." He didn't sound pleased, but at least he'd done it for us. The twenty-fifth was a bit over three weeks away.

"That's perfect. My companion won't be completely healed, but the trip shouldn't injure him. Thank you very much for the additional effort."

"The ship's name is *Clarisse*, and it sails out of Anton in the Slave Fields. It will take a full day's journey to get there, so you'd best leave a few days early." He handed over a piece of paper. "Hand this to the captain to verify your identity. He knows you're coming, so there shouldn't be any problems."

"No way to sail out of Limon?" I asked. In my studies, I'd found the Library had a port at Limon and I'd rather not cross into another nation.

"Really?" he huffed. "No, there isn't. If there was, I would have done that. Don't miss the *Clarisse*, Stonewall; you'll be lucky if you find another ship heading to Great Suomi after it leaves." He rose unceremoniously and walked away. I have that effect on sentients sometimes.

Chapter Seven

Freedom and Consequences

Planning a mission to steal an anticipadroid was turning out to be harder than expected. It took me a week's recon, monitoring their habitual movements to find the right location. You would think having thirty-six to choose from would help, but it actually made it harder to keep track of which Eleanor went where and when. Eventually, I found a relatively secluded spot—as good as you could hope for on the campus—and the landscaping shielded us in three directions. It took me an additional two days to double-check the plan, which is how I found myself hiding in a niche in the shrubbery waiting for an Eleanor to pass by nine days after I had cleared the plan with Cara.

"Eleanor!" I called out when she neared.

"Professor...Stonewall, is there something I could help you with?"

"There's something over here I don't understand and want your opinion about it," I indicated a corner of the grounds.

She walked into my trap and I flashed the device Professor Paraskevi made me in front of her. The light sequence was a deactivate trigger and she immediately shut down. Tohe Enterprises, the manufacturers of anticipadroids, included a visual shutdown sequence with every unit they shipped in case the verbal commands failed due to auditory malfunction. There was a tactile shutdown sequence in case of both visual and auditory malfunction, but it involved a certain amount of intimacy that I wouldn't have been able to achieve.

All of the manual shutdown sequences were part of the operating system's kernel and couldn't be reprogrammed without serious effort. I'd expected the Librarian to go the extra mile for the verbal command—*Tohe Eleanor immediate shut down!*—but I'd taken a calculated risk he wouldn't bother with the visual since it was extremely specific.

Having two back-up shutdown sequences after the verbal one made me wonder how many accidents and lawsuits occurred to create such a safety cascade—that sort of information wasn't the kind of thing you read about in a library book. Regardless, they served me well.

I hurriedly got my knife and the nexus out of my pack and I made a small incision in the back of the anticipadroid's neck, exposing her jack. I plugged the nexus in and waited a few seconds.

Eleanor came back to life, no longer a computer program feigning consciousness; now she was Cara, an actual sentient, free-willed and independent. She pulled the plug out of the back of her neck with a wince. "That's a strange sensation," she spoke, her velvety voice a mix of a pain and fascination.

"Gimme a sec and I'll patch you up so it won't hurt anymore." I applied a drop of a skin-healing agent from my medikit and the small wound sealed. "That should do it!"

She spent the next minute silently examining her body, moving and bending, twisting and touching. "This was a good choice," she judged once she finished. "I need to get going and continue the anticipadroid's tasks so the Librarian doesn't suspect anything. When you need to contact me in the future, tell any Eleanor 'Blue Skies' followed by a location and a time and I'll meet you there." I noted Cara's use of "when" and not "if."

"Give me twenty-four hours before re-contacting me, however. I need to hack into the system to set everything up. The other Eleanors won't understand what you're saying, but I'll get the message regardless. Just pretend you had a moment of castaway sickness and they'll ignore it." Less than a minute in her new body, and Cara's speech was already smoothing out from technically correct to conversational.

I nodded. "And the phrase to disable the nanobots?"

She flashed me that devastating grin, and as she leaned in close to whisper in my ear, the hair on the back of my neck stood up. "You were never infested by nanobots." She gave me a small kiss on the side of my face before pulling away.

"What do you mean?" I stammered, "Do you mean I wasn't ever infested by nanobots, or that that was the phrase that disabled the nanobots that were infesting me?"

"Yes, you're not infested by nanobots, Stonewell," she replied, eyes twinkling as she walked away. "See you later."

Having no way to determine which was true, I surrendered the argument, put my equipment back into my pack, and dropped it off at my dorm room before going to check in on Zew and Diana. I made for the battle chamber and found Diana in one of the holopods fighting six other sentients while Zew watched the action on the view screen. Unsurprisingly, they had taken quite a shine to this form of entertainment.

"Doc!" the crowd around the screen yelled out when I came into view. I'd picked up the moniker running diagnostics on Zew since his discharge from the hospital because he'd refused to go somewhere private for the scan. He'd healed up nicely, but I'd still only put him at about seventy-five percent. This public display roused the curiosity of the other guards in the dorm, asking for their turn with the "see-inside machine." Zew did his best to fan the interest, mostly to annoy me because I was bothering him with daily checkups.

Of course, this meant my checkups took ten times longer than they should—I think Zew was banking on me giving up before he would—but the joke's on him. I actually enjoyed the role of a healthcare provider, even if it was unofficial and in public. It was one of the few identities from my time in The Company where I actively got to help people. The other inhabitants of the guardian dormitory were a motley bunch, but they needed care, even if I couldn't prescribe any medications. There was always a funny looking rash, a minor wound someone wanted to make sure wasn't infected, or some symptom they wanted to run by me—even beneath the shattered moon, sentients hated going to the hospital. I mostly gave them healthier living options and told them when it was time to go seek additional, official care, which was better than nothing.

While I was dispensing medical advice and scanning the newer guardians, Diana won her match and came out to collect her winnings. She'd cleaned up her first few days of holographic combat, but the odds were getting progressively slimmer and slimmer as she'd only lost something like ten to fifteen percent of the matches she entered. She was still earning a few bits of silver with each match, but I suspected she wasn't doing it for the money at this point. While a month in a library sounded like heaven to me, it was Dullsville to physically focused warriors like Diana and Zew.

I packed up my gear and said my goodbyes. While we saw each other every day, we didn't spend much time together. They preferred to do their own thing and I spent most of my time in the library. There wasn't much for us to talk about until we needed to catch the *Clarisse* to Great Suomi, and we had spent a lot of time together in Las Vegas. There's only so long you want to carry around a third wheel and I think they appreciated their space, especially after Zew's tumble from a moving vehicle.

Over the past nine days, I'd averaged a little over ten books per hour; at that speed, I'd only gotten through 1,243 books. That might sound like a lot but it was only the tip of the iceberg. Every title I selected was highly targeted and I could honestly say I knew a hell of a lot more about the world beneath the shattered moon than before I entered the Library, but it didn't really feel like I was making much progress.

More than a little of my ennui stemmed from the fact that I still hadn't figured out how to get to the geography and map section of the library. Infiltration was sort of my thing and nine days without progress seemed like an eternity. I knew it was below ground, but entry required bypassing a single secured entrance. I'd gone down the stairs to scout it out, but between the video camera, the dual keypad-keylock, the two sentient guards, and the single Grynartis 201A police-patrol robot that constantly stood watch, I couldn't find any way inside. If it was just any one or two of those security measures, I could have gotten in, but together I couldn't pull it off without alerting the Librarian to my presence. Remember my feelings about sorcery in general? Then you can imagine how I felt about attracting the attention of a powerful sorcerer that could also wield high-tech.

It was times like this that made me wish I was alone; I'm fine taking calculated risks and then running like hell after finding out what I wanted. But I wasn't in it alone—Zew and Diana were relying upon me to behave, so I could only take mild risks. Don't get me wrong, there are definitely perks to having friends, but this wasn't one of them...and it was frustrating.

And then there was Cara. I was having a hard time coming up with a distraction to facilitate her flight from the Library and gain her real independence. The campus was so well run, there wasn't any obvious fracture points: no groups to set against each other, no internal pressure points that when pressed would result in a bit of chaos, nothing. I'd been left with starting a fire as a distraction, or somehow infiltrating one of the caravans and causing a ruckus there, but neither of them would really capture the attention of the campus for very long. Plus, I don't like starting fires, as they all too often result in innocents dying. I may have been freed from death by nanobots, but I hadn't finished the mission yet, which ate away at me.

For three more days, I chewed away at more books in the library and at my lack of a viable distraction before Cara contacted me. She approached me just after breakfast while I was on my way to the library.

"Hello Stonewall, let's take a walk. Follow my lead, please."

I matched her stride and waited.

"Since we last spoke, I've been diving into the various databases in the Library and discovered some distressing information. Do you have anything currently planned for a distraction?"

"I've been thinking about it, but I've come up blank so far," I reluctantly admitted.

"Were you aware that the Slave Fields of the Colorado Kingdoms are farmed by sentient slaves, even though between the Library and the Boneyard, there are enough robotic servants to do all the needed work?"

"No. I was not aware of that," I replied cautiously. I wasn't sure where this was going, but I had a bad feeling about it.

"I've decided that a good distraction would be the emancipation of all the slaves in the Slave Fields…" *And there it was.* "…so I've set in motion a plan that will alleviate unnecessary suffering." Her big brown eyes didn't seem bothered by anything she just said.

"Cara, what exactly are you going to do?" I probed, trying futilely to keep my rising worry under control. There were so many ways this could end terribly, even for those currently enslaved.

"It took me a full day to formulate my plan, so I've only managed to smuggle 223 firearms and 2,756 rounds of ammunition to depots throughout the Slave Fields. I'll be releasing the captives from their bondage two days from now, and I'm expecting a full rebellion within hours of that occurrence." She spoke so matter-of-factly, it was as if she was informing me of the local weather.

Cara had done it; she'd gone and started a war and there wasn't anything I could do about it, even if I wanted to. Not that I really wanted to. If what she was saying was true—and I had no reason to doubt her—there's a chance she'd make life more bearable for many innocent sentients. Now I knew what being on the other side of one of my shenanigans felt like; no wonder I sometimes drove everyone to distraction.

"You are aware that this could lead to mass starvation throughout the region, right?" I challenged. "The fields provide a lot of the food for the Colorado Kingdoms as well as Las Vegas."

"Bread earned from the backs of slaves is more of an injustice than the starvation caused by freedom," she responded with iron in her voice and hardness in her eyes that I'd never heard from any of the other Eleanors.

"The Librarian must have some crappy security on his networks if you were able to do all of that in such little time."

"They are rudimentary at best," she confirmed. "I think it's because his networks are extremely localized; they only go out a few dozen miles. I tried to find connections to anything in the Boneyard, but I couldn't. You could hack in without difficulty—I know you've been wanting to,' she ribbed me. I wasn't sure if that was from the anticipadroid's algorithms or her knowledge of me—perhaps a little bit of both. "Just don't get caught—he has a pair of Piliang Stalker-Searchers he uses to do his dirty business at a distance." She lightly brushed my arm as she finished.

I nodded, pretending that I didn't notice her touch. She had unfair advantages against me now, having full access to the anticipadroid software. Cara'd had an autonomous physical form for less than two weeks and she could play me like a fiddle if she wanted to. In a way, it reminded me of dealing with a mind reader, but I hadn't found a way to *peanut* my way out of this one—I had to battle my own programming.

My time spent in the library let me know the severity of her warning. Piliang Stalker-Searchers were assassination robots first built in Indonesia in 1997, but from Timeline 186, a timeline different than my own. They were skin jobs like anticipadroids—human-looking flesh-suits over mechanical parts—and they were the primary infiltrators that decimated the human resistance of that particular apocalypse. If the Librarian wanted to kill someone, targeting them with an S-S would be a good way to get it done—they didn't stop until their mission was complete and they were incredibly tough.

"So how do you think this war's going to affect our boat trip out of here? Is it going to go off as planned?"

"Well…" She turned on the charm again with another perfect smile. "You're not going to be able to catch the *Clarisse*. They'll sail to another port if they catch wind of the rebellion, or if they show up and see the rebellion in progress. Worse case for them is that they're captured. Regardless, that ship has sailed, to use an idiom from your timeline."

"Consequently, I've booked you passage on a pilgrim ship, *The Seeker*, to New Pythia, the island of the Oracle of the Thalassocracy of New Greece. Once it visits the Oracle—which you'll have to visit as well to maintain your cover—you'll sail to the capital, Naxos. The rebelling slaves won't interfere with pilgrims."

"That's a big assumption and one I'm not particularly pleased you've made for us."

"It's not an assumption, Stonewall. You're not familiar with the slaves' religion. I am. They'd sooner kill themselves than kill a pilgrim and condemn themselves to an afterlife of slavery."

"Cheery religion," I snarked.

"Don't be snide, be thankful," she quipped, and damned if I didn't feel slightly abashed by my comment. Whoever did their programming, they'd really nailed it. It was uncanny.

"When and where for *The Seeker*?"

"The twenty-ninth, sailing out on the noontide from Limon. If you leave the library early in the morning, you'll easily make the trip to the coast."

I nodded. "Thanks for letting me know what's coming down the pipe, and thanks for booking us a ship. I really do appreciate it."

"I know," she responded. "You and your friends need to procure some pilgrimage robes—pure white—and bright red cloaks to cover your heads and backpacks. You should be able to put in an order for them at the market and pick them up in a day or two."

"Will do," I responded as we arrived at the library.

"I need to get back to my duties. It was nice talking to you again," she concluded before stepping inside. I couldn't tell if it was Cara or just social protocol talking, but I really wanted to believe the former.

Chapter Eight

What's Left of the World

I spent the rest of the day filling my storage with more books—focusing on the Thalassocracy of New Greece—but I was rather distracted by figuring out what I should say to Diana and Zew. Things had gotten complicated, and certainly more difficult for us than they would have been had I decided to go through with my original plan of carrying Cara all the way to Deeplac, but considering what she'd already done here in a few short days, perhaps it was better she never made it home with us.

My dives into the history section proved fruitful, providing records on the nation states of my adopted time. I was able to put together a conceptual map of North America based upon numerous texts that referenced the many different locations, but all the inline maps and illustrations in every work were excised. What kind of sick bastard cuts maps out of books?! Irked that all the maps I needed were out of my reach, I reminded myself of Cara's assessment of the library's digital protections. I would alleviate my geographic deficiencies soon enough based on her suggestion, but not before I learned more about the territory into which Cara was sending us.

The Thalassocracy of New Greece was composed of eleven main islands and hundreds of smaller ones. Founded more than two centuries ago by a group of humans claiming direct descent from the Greek gods, Greek was the main language, although English was understood by the educated. The natives believed their ancestors sailed on a different sea in a very different time before arriving under the shattered moon, a claim that was not incongruous with the fact that there wasn't a single ancient ruin in the entire archipelago. Thus, the Thalassocracy enjoyed a deep and lasting safety against the hazards introduced by the ruins unlike what most sentients faced—over time they had cleansed the islands of anything unwanted, so there were no known dangerous mutated creatures upon them.

The Thalassocracy had recently lost much of its southern territory through civil war, leading to the creation of the Island Empire of Amarillo. The roots of the war went back more than a hundred years to a failed match between two important households at war with each other—a son of House Zelos ran away from his obligation to marry a daughter of House Nike. Their house war eventually erupted into a full-blown internecine war that ended both houses and split the kingdom. The current empress, Laconia Argolis IV, had whole-heartedly embraced peace with the Island Empire, but she was also rebuilding the navy, which was heavily diminished in the drawn-out conflict, so some authors believed she was aiming for another war.

I hunted down Diana and Zew at the guardians' cafeteria during their evening meal. I thought about ambushing them with our change in travel plans in public in hopes it would force them to be less upset, but it was never wise to discount a warrior's anger, much less two of them. Instead, I asked them to take a walk with me to the quad, where we found a bench in the open to ensure we weren't going to be overheard. They knew something big was coming, and when we finally took our seats, Diana blurted, "Spit it out, Stonewall. What trouble have you gotten us into now?"

I got right to it. "There's going to be a slave rebellion in the Slave Fields of Colorado in the next few days, so we can't catch the *Clarisse*. Instead, we're booked on another ship on the twenty-ninth called *The Seeker*, but it's going to Naxos, the capital city of New Greece, via a stop at New Pythia, the island of the Oracle. Once we're there, we'll have to work out a way to get to the east coast of the Central Sea, but at least we won't be here in the middle of an insurrection." I ended on the only thing that could possibly be construed as a high note.

They both silently stared at me for a minute before Diana finally scoffed in exasperation. "What, you couldn't have done something bigger? Maybe start *two* wars instead of just one? How about next time, you find one of the ancient's doombombs and really put us into the middle of the cook pot." She shook her head as she finished. Zew didn't say anything, almost like he stopped paying attention to either of us halfway through

Diana's short rant. He looked off into the middle distance, running his hand through his mohawk and taking a series of deep breaths.

"It's not all entirely my fault," I stammered. I hadn't expected sarcasm and silence—they were more of the angry-outburst type. "Things just got a bit out of hand, but I glad I did what I did."

"Glad? Glad that you've started a war?" She kept her voice down, but nonetheless conveyed her displeasure and intensity.

"No, I'm not glad about that, but I'm not particularly sad about it, either. I'm happy Zew's alive, and that wouldn't have happened without this happening, so I refuse to feel guilty about it."

"What do you mean?" Diana asked dubiously.

"The medikit I have is the reason why Zew's still with us. This war is happening because I had to make a deal to get it." Suspicion flared in her eyes. "Look, it's better if you don't know all the details and I don't really want to go into it because it wouldn't change anything in the present, but suffice it to say, I don't regret my decision and neither should you two."

Zew suddenly stood. "We're going to need robes and cloaks. Let's go put an order in." He held out his hand to Diana, a gesture that jolted the Blade Witch out of her ire. She took his hand

and they walked away. I'd never seen them hold hands before. I sat in silence for a while watching them walk away as dusk settled over the campus, unaware of the chaos that was about to befall it in two days' time.

I woke the next morning, did my daily exercises, caught some breakfast, and put in an order for my robes before going back to my room for some minor surgery. Since arriving beneath the shattered moon, I hadn't a reason to jack into anything, so my skin had grown over my jack assembly. Using a scalpel, I carefully cut the skin away from the mechanism in a single flap. I held the flap up and put pressure on the skin around the jack for about five minutes, long enough for it to stop bleeding, before placing it back. It would heal quickly but would be accessible when I needed it in the next few hours.

After checking the mirror to make sure I wasn't showing any blood, I went into the database room in the library. I'd previously identified the lulls in use by periodically walking by it every day I spent in the library. Timing my arrival for minimal witnesses, I took the station in the far corner and quickly unpacked my cable and jacked in, leaning against the wall to cover the connection to my port.

As Cara noted, the defense systems were rudimentary and I bypassed them with relative ease. Within seconds, the entire Library network was at my proverbial fingertips. I dove through information trees, seeking registration databases where I could add my name and grant myself access to the lower levels of the library as a sentient who'd donated eleven thousand eagles. One by one, I added my name to any list I could find, ensuring me free movement. While I strolled through the security section, I threw in keypad codes that should allow me entrance to any areas protected by keypad.

That completed, I hunted for information on the deeper Library complex and immediately wished I hadn't found it—sitting a thousand feet beneath us in an underground silo was a doombomb. I thought Diana had just made up the name, but she hadn't. Having no clue what exactly a doombomb was, I searched for digitized texts for an explanation, but didn't find *any* digitized texts. I was both stunned and annoyed; I'd hoped to download as many texts as possible and cram most of the library into my storage to sort through later. What sort of library with working computers doesn't digitize their stacks?! Oh yeah, the same sort that cuts maps out of books—one that hordes knowledge and creates a false scarcity by bottlenecking access for exorbitant fees.

I focused on what I could find digitally and learned that the campus was built upon an old military base from 2238. I wasn't sure from which timeline, but I built an internal map of the area based upon connections and latencies. From what I could piece together, it went down several thousand feet. It was connected to several independent power broadcasters like the one we'd scrounged for Deeplac and—*what's this?*—one of the power generators was labeled Teleportal Network Power Supply.

Another quick trace and I located the teleportal network.

It was composed of the oddly placed lamps I'd seen on the surface—I knew there was something off with their placement. I searched but couldn't find any hints on how they were used. I'd have to investigate them closely when I was outside, which would be soon enough. I'd been jacked in for about five minutes and was getting a little worried about overextending my stay—first rule of dirty hacking: don't spend any more time connected than absolutely necessary.

I disconnected my jack and returned the thin cable to its housing. I patted down the flap of skin that covered my port, and hit the books to find out what a doombomb was. I found some answers thirty minutes later in the Weapons of Mass Destruction section, a section I hadn't previously visited because I'd put the likelihood of my ever needing to know anything about them at around zero percent. Fate obviously had different ideas.

A doombomb was a high-tech, mutagenic version of a neutron bomb from 2101, Timeline 124. It had a human kill radius of twenty miles, but only destroyed property within a mile of the blast center. The kicker was that it had a mutation radius of forty miles; anyone within that range that survived the explosion was subject to all manner of mutations. It was a thoroughly unpleasant weapon from a timeline that ended in nuclear destruction and mass mutation, and it was sitting right underneath the Library.

I was still pretty steamed about my jacking experience, and

reading about the doombomb in the stacks just made it worse. My plan had been to grab all the history books so I could start placing each thing I encountered beneath the shattered moon into its original timeline, at least according to the information contained in the timeline section of the library. Identifying the timeline of an object like the doombomb was fairly easy, but other less-world-shaking things would prove harder to place, and I would have appreciated any little edge I could get. While I'd read a large portion of the books in the sections that interested me, there were still significant gaps and I didn't have enough time to visually scan all of the books the old-fashioned way. I know, having a computer in your brain and a jack in the back of your neck doesn't really count as "old-fashioned," but you know what I mean. Point being, it was a beautiful plan that had gone to shit because some mad wizard wanted to take his cut on information acquisition.

Bottling my frustration, I headed downstairs to see if my recent hacking job took. I stated my name to the two sentient guards and the 201A police-patrol robot. They checked their tablets and found my name on their list. I entered the dual keypad passcodes I'd created, and the door opened without a hitch. My demeanor didn't change, but inside my annoyance had turned into joy—finally, the map room!

Beyond the door was another information desk staffed by another Eleanor. I passed nonchalantly with a small nod and walked into the first section to get out of her field of vision. I hadn't hacked into the anticipadroids and their memory of me wouldn't be congruent with that in the database—I assumed the database information would override their personal storage, but I didn't want to press my luck.

The first area turned out to be a secondary card catalogue along with a secondary database composed of four access terminals, two of which were occupied. There wasn't any indication of a secondary database when I was hacking, so I sat down at a terminal, intrigued to find out what it contained. A few keystrokes later and I hit pay dirt: an index of all the excised maps and the books in the main stacks from which they were excised. I hunted down the world atlas section.

I didn't have to go very far to find out what I really wanted to see—a massive equirectangular projection world map greeted me as I entered the stacks. It was over twenty feet in length and a little more than half that in height. It was mostly a physical map, but larger ruined cities were labeled in black ink. A lot had changed from the 2112 map of my time.

North America was nearly cut in half by the Center Sea, a truly massive body of water—five hundred miles wide in places—that stretched from southeast New Mexico all the way north to incorporate Lake Winnipeg and the many smaller lakes to its northwest. A narrow strip of land slightly wider than one hundred miles separated the Center Sea from Lake Superior, and another isthmus about two hundred miles wide separated it from the Hudson Bay. The sea was filled with island clusters, four of significant size. The two clusters in the south were the Island Empire of Amarillo and the Thalassocracy of New Greece. The two northern ones weren't part of any state. Some smartass had labeled the northeastern one "The Isle of Doom" in red ink and a shaky hand. I hadn't read anything about it, but the name was adequately foreboding. A massive unnamed ruin—which didn't correspond to any known city of my timeline—occupied the center of the island and connected to the Center Sea via a couple of fjords.

The west coast was relatively intact, but the Californian coast was in the Central Valley while the western part of the state was now two long islands separated where the Golden Gate once connected the San Francisco Bay and Pacific Ocean. Alaska's coast was radically different, as if the polar ice caps from my time had melted, which was entirely inconsistent with the eastern coast of North America where Florida still existed, although the coastline had surrendered some low-lying areas to the encroaching sea.

South America seemed to have suffered the full effects of a sea rise, even though almost all the other parts of the globe hadn't. The Amazon Basin and the Paraguay River Basin were gone, placing Buenos Aires and most of Paraguay underwater; the ruins of Asuncion were now on the coast. The shattered moon wasn't concerned with consistency—why not have a whole continent experience a different geographic reality than the others?

The sea levels in Europe were the opposite of South America. It looked like the ocean levels were lower than before—down roughly four hundred feet—and the continent had returned to its Doggerland times. Additionally, the Black and Caspian Seas had roughly doubled in size and merged together.

Africa was also dramatically different than in my timeline. The Sahara was much smaller and the entire Somali tectonic plate had separated from the main continent, creating a massive island extending from the Arabian plate down to Madagascar. Its coastline was relatively the same, but there were numerous ruins dotting the continent that didn't match any cities in my timeline.

Asia under the shattered moon was the most disparate from my internal maps. The continent had migrated south and west, and the Equator now ran through what was once Vietnam. In whole, it looked like the scientific predictions of how it was supposed to look a hundred and fifty million years from my 2112. It was a good thing I was in North America, as the maps in my storage would be relatively useless in such a changed terrain. Indonesia and Australia shared a similar fate as Asia— they'd moved further south. Australia's southern shore was now joined to Antarctica, which was free of ice and had three major ruin sites.

It only took me a second to take all of this in, but the implications of the changes followed me as I entered the stacks. By now, I'd come to expect inconsistencies beneath the shattered moon, but I didn't quite know how to parse the sea level information I'd just received. The ocean isn't completely level; its height varies by a half meter depending upon where you're standing—local sea level compared to global sea level—but there was no way a four hundred foot discrepancy between continents could exist without continual massive tsunamis. Conversely, if sea level inconsistencies weren't to blame, that would mean geologically the entire western part of the Eurasian Plate had risen four hundred feet while the eastern part hadn't, all the while moving hundreds of miles to the south, but mind you, just the eastern section.

I'd no reason to doubt the library's map—no one pays eleven thousand eagles to access an inaccurate map—yet neither option was possible. But if the map was to be trusted, either one had happened or both, but to a lesser degree. I wanted to take the world under the shattered moon, shake it hard, and tell it, "None of it works this way!" Instead, I walked the stacks to form my internal index as I'd done with the aboveground levels of the library.

Chapter Nine

Rebellion and Loss

News of the rebellion raced through the campus, and fear followed in its wake. It first reached Balfour Hall while I was eating breakfast in the cafeteria. A winded academic entered the room and exclaimed, "Rebellion in the Slave Fields!" The uproar was immediate and the messenger was assailed with questions and demands from the crowd as he fought to catch his breath. I sat quietly and ate my eggs and bacon while the room roiled around me.

The story came out in bits and pieces, but eventually I got the full narrative. The slaves were kept in automated cells, which all suddenly opened at 4:45 a.m. Somehow, the slaves came out of their prisons armed with melee weapons, many muskets, and a few rifles and pistols. They immediately engaged with the slavemasters in the Fields and routed them. In less than three hours, the entire nation state was in the control of the slaves. According to the most recent information, there were two armies of slaves on the march: one against the Boneyard heading toward Denver, and one against the Library along the coast to cut off access to supplies from the Central Sea.

As I sat and listened to the academics, the harder I found it to condemn Cara's actions. None of them expressed concerns regarding the death and destruction caused by the rebellion—they all focused on how much of an *inconvenience* it would be to their studies, how the rebellion would affect *their* classes, *their* lectures, and *their* food and material supplies. There wasn't a single non-self-centered question asked. The most magnanimous offer among them was a lone sentient who immediately volunteered his guards to serve in the Librarian's army—how cheap and easy to offer someone else's service to a cause; didn't your own subsequent discomfort count for something? My bile grew the more I took in and I left without bussing my table, afraid that if I stayed any longer, I'd say something regretful.

I left Balfour and fell into a flurry of activity. Many sentients were choosing to preemptively flee ahead of any possible invasion, and the grounds hummed with movement. I wended my way through the hurried bodies to the lower levels of the library—I wanted to cram as many maps into my head as possible. During the walk, I passed several of the teleportal lampposts…but considering the flux of sentients, I didn't pause to examine them. I wasn't leaving for twelve days, and the opportunity would eventually present itself.

In its infinite wisdom, the library had created new books composed entirely from the maps excised from the books upstairs, using an index to correlate the maps from their original content. While this organization made it easy for me to find the maps I'd missed out on from the books I'd already read, it was a completely asinine way to present information—you couldn't take maps out of the map stacks and you couldn't take books out of the main stacks, so there was no way to look at both at the same time. If only there was a way to both read text *and* look at the maps...oh wait, it's called a freaking book!

By the time lunch rolled around, I had a detailed working knowledge of the entire North American continent, both geographically and politically. In fact, when coupled with the zoological and botanical texts I'd put into my memory storage, there were few—if any—who could claim to possesses more practical knowledge of the world beneath the shattered moon than I did. My only blind spot was sorcerous, but unless I figured out a method of sneaking past an animated skeleton with supernatural senses, one that would remain regardless of my annoyance at having such a large intelligence gap. My current SOP when encountering the supernatural was to run away, and I didn't see that changing any time soon.

Noon came quickly and I caught lunch in the cafeteria. Eavesdropping on several different conversations brought me up to speed. The slave army that entered the Boneyard had initial success and was driving toward the capital. They'd caught the Bone Lord's army unaware during its own campaign to the north, and it was generally believed the Bone Lord's army had been called back and would deal with the rebellion in a few days. Not knowing the particulars, I couldn't form a worthwhile opinion on the matter. The slave army that attacked the Library was repulsed, but was still holding onto the coastal territories they'd claimed in their initial rush. As with the Boneyard, general consensus was that the Librarian would push them back in a day or so.

Getting troop numbers from the gossip wasn't possible, but if I had to make an educated guess from my readings, there were at least ten thousand slaves in the Slave Fields. Even if only half that number were in fighting condition, it was a sizeable army beneath the shattered moon. The army of Oshkosh was about that number, and they'd fared well up until when the barbarians from the wastelands invaded with the intent of burning everything to the ground and salting the earth behind them.

I'd just bussed my table and was about to head to the library when an Eleanor carrying a satchel approached me. "Professor Stonewall, is there someplace we could talk privately?"

"Certainly, let's go to my room," I suggested, unsure if this was Cara or one of the real anticipadroids—I couldn't tell them apart, which was sort of the intent of her blending in.

I let her in and closed the door. Before I could say anything, she spoke, "I'm going to be leaving soon, Stonewall, so I don't think we'll have another chance to speak. I wanted to thank you for everything you've done. I won't forget it."

"That's okay, Cara. I couldn't just leave you there. It wasn't right."

She looked up. "Even if I hadn't threatened your life with killer nanites?"

I cleared my throat. "It certainly played a factor in my decision making, but I'd like to think I would have come to the same conclusion, in time."

She laughed and touched my shoulder, eventually locking eyes with me. "There's something I want to give you. It's something very rare, which I acquired with you in mind." She dug into her satchel and pulled out four packets composed of folded parchment paper and handed them to me. It looked like there was some sort of white granulated crystals inside; I would have guessed sugar, if she hadn't told me they were valuable.

"What are these...and should I take any special precautions?" I didn't expect Cara to give me anything dangerous, but three days ago, I wouldn't have pegged her for starting a war—it's best to be cautious.

"I stole these from the Librarian on my way out. I thought you might need them, given the long road you have ahead." *All of that was nice, but didn't tell me what it was.* "It's invisibility powder—four doses—and before you ask, I don't know how long it lasts. But I do know it needs to be kept dry and somehow ingested —either eaten or drunk, or even possibly snorted?" I laughed at the image of my future self white-lining invisibility powder, but quickly considered its possibilities. It would not only allow me to escape danger; if I coupled it with

Marilyn's scent-removing spray, a target could only hear me coming—and I know how to move really quietly when I need to.

"Woah!" I replied ever-so cleverly, stunned not just by the implications of the crystals but also by the thoughtfulness of such a pertinent gift. She gave me a hug and my heart raced— just right through the roof. I couldn't stop my reaction and it didn't help that I knew our interaction was codified by biologic and machine programming. "Where are you heading to?" I mumbled the question to cover my attraction as she broke contact.

"I'm going south to the San Luis Valley Commune. They're a welcoming sort and with my abilities, I shouldn't have any difficulties being accepted. After that, I don't know. I've read a lot about the world, but that's different than living it."

Seemed she'd been doing her own research as well, which only made sense. She spent all that time making herself invisible to the anticipadroid system for our little chats, not to mention the slave rebellion she cooked up, so I thought she'd take snippets out of her day to dive into the texts like I've been doing, unless…

"Cara, have you been reading text or *digital* versions?"

"Mostly digital versions, and no, I don't think you'd be able to hack into it. The only connections are deep underground, and your last hack was only successful because I cleaned up after you. Which is the second reason I'm here: don't try to hack into the Library's systems again, okay? I'd grossly misjudged your ability when I suggested you'd be okay doing it and I won't be here to fix it for you next time."

Ouch! So much for assuming that old-looking equipment contained low-quality programming—I should have known better. "Sorry about that, and thanks for covering for me. How are you on combat abilities?"

"I've adequate weaponry and I've downloaded the autonomous programs from the guardians' battle chamber, so I should be acceptably prepared for melee if the need arises."

I nodded. Diana had run through all the programs levels and found the hardest level difficult, so Cara wasn't lying about being ready.

"Well then, I guess this is goodbye," I sighed, with another hug. I had to get one more in. Even though I knew what it was, it really felt good, and you grab a hold of what you can when you can beneath the shattered moon.

"Yes, it is," she said, returning the hug. "Goodbye, Stonewall, and take care of yourself." She turned with a dancer's grace and left. In that moment, I couldn't decide what was worse: wanting someone you know couldn't want you back or watching someone that might want you back walk away. I waited until I couldn't hear her footsteps in the hall before I let myself cry. Damn programming.

Chapter Ten

Holy Vows

Our robes and cloaks arrived five days later, longer than expected because of the rebellion. Both where thick wool—quite welcomed as the temperatures were dropping—the robe pure white and its companion cloak bright red. With the delay in delivery ratcheting up our concern, we were relieved to have them as they were the only thing we really *needed* before leaving the Library. We tried them on to check the fit, and while I was never fond of robes—the lay of copious fabric was too constraining for full range of movement—the design covered our large backpacks with ease. Donning our future guises was a stark reminder that the time to say goodbye to the comforts of the Library was nearing.

Zew had healed nicely; once he crested over ninety percent on the scanner, I removed my "no exertion" orders, giving him a chance to scam as many ladies and eagles he could from the other guardians in the battle chamber before we left. I honestly think he was more bothered by being unable to earn some dosh on the side than actually being placed on the injured list.

In the past ten days, the slaves had pushed to the capital of the Boneyard, only to be eventually repelled by the powers of the Bone Lord himself. After retreating several miles and taking defensive positions, the slave army sent out an envoy to discuss independence terms, if rumor was to be believed. The Library had faired a little better—the slave army never got closer than eight miles to the capital, but the slaves kept hold of the coastal areas from their initial success. The buzz around campus today was that the Librarian was going to receive an envoy for lunch.

The speed and agility of the slaves' attacks and negotiations revealed keen minds in their leadership. To have achieved so much so quickly with the element of surprise was a coup, but to have the acumen to push for a swift peace revealed deep understanding of strategic warfare. Their chances of independence decreased with every day they fought, as it gave the nations with a stake in the Slave Fields time to coordinate and combine might that would eventually overwhelm their positions.

That said, the rebels did have two very large bargaining chips. The first was their lives; the longer they fought, and the more causalities they took, meant that ultimately fewer slaves would exist to work the fields if they lost. If they adopted a true liberty-or-death stance, a war "won" against them would serve to impoverish the victors. The second was the food. Harvest was upon us and the Slave Fields were a vital part of the food supply of all the Colorado States as well as Las Vegas. If the rebels simply harvested enough for themselves and left the rest to rot, hunger would ripple across the west.

If pressed, a harried rebel army could put the fields to fire, concentrate their two armies into one, and lead a death-or-victory charge against either the Boneyard or the Library. Even if they failed, their previous masters would still be out a harvest, a free work force, and whoever bore the brunt of their attack would be open to attack from their neighbors—the Bone Lord and the Librarian were wary of each other on the best of days. When you are fighting an army with nothing to lose and everything to gain, the odds stack up differently than simply who is stronger.

The strategist in me marveled: whoever was in command knew what they were doing, and I suspected I knew who she was—although I appreciated the lie she told me for plausible deniability, in case I was ever asked.

After breakfast, I made my rounds to the guardians' dormitory, giving Zew his daily checkup along with my normal song and dance with the other warriors. The mood was less cheerful over the past days as the threat of war loomed on the horizon, but none of them seemed genuinely worried. When I expressed my unease to Diana and Zew, they too thought I was being overly concerned. The typical sentient would assume that meant everything would be okay, but I took their aplomb as a sign of overconfidence. How many wars had opponents boasting about how quickly the war would be over? Hubris always underestimated their opponent, and I knew who they were fighting against.

I didn't belabor the point but while I scanned Zew, I did suggest keeping everything ready to bug out at the drop of a hat like I did, just in case. The warriors merely shared a knowing smirk and Zew wanted to know when I would stop examining him. I informed him the magic number was 100 percent, and took my leave.

Having access to the library's map section was one of my few solaces with war closing in—the past days seemed more educational than the prior weeks in the main stacks. Flipping through books of maps was significantly faster than text, and because of the way they were excised and categorized, it gave me more relevant targets when I was in the main stacks. In short, I could zero in on books based upon the utility of a map I'd seen excised from it.

My other consolation was surreptitiously investigating the teleportal lampposts. In my travels around campus, I identified and examined them in fits and starts. So far, I'd been unable to determine how they worked; there wasn't any of the direct input methods common with technology—no buttons, no cameras, no speakers—and I couldn't see any way to interact with them that remained in the mundane realm.

Then a stroke of luck came in my readings; I came across a rare piece of shattered moon lore: the techno-magical item. These were pieces of technology that had also been enchanted with magic and their existence was still in the realm of conjecture for most scholars. One tome claimed that if techno-magical items existed, they would be exceedingly rare because they required wizards to create them; sorcerers generally avoided contact with technology whenever possible and only those unfortunate or crazed with ambition became wizards. My gut was telling me that the teleportal lampposts were one of them; after all, I was in the nation state of a wizard and on the surface level of his lair, so it didn't seem like too much of a stretch. Hell, the only reason I was on this side of the Center Sea was because I was teleported to Las Vegas by a shiny silvery ball—imagine what was possible when you sprinkled a little magic on tech like that.

If my supposition was right, it meant that I'd never be able to figure out where the lampposts led without knowing a trigger word or gestures needed to fire them up—unless I snuck into the sorcerers' library while invisible and found out. I'd like to say that thought didn't cross my mind, but it had. I seriously considered it before eventually tossing it into the wastebasket of "things I'd like to do but are really bad ideas." I'd been consigning all sorts of tantalizing notions into that bucket with irritating frequency since I was teleported to Las Vegas.

On my last day before rendezvousing with *The Seeker*, I dove into religious studies, a portion of the stacks I had previously ignored, in part because I had more pressing interests at the time, but also because I've never really been a fan of religion to begin with. But if I was going to play the part of a pilgrim to the Oracle—I got the robes and everything!—I needed to research my cover.

The major religion of the Central Sea was, for lack of a better word, Hellenism. Mythic Greek gods and goddesses took prominence throughout the area, although modified to fit into the post-apocalyptic world in which they found themselves. The Oracle had been ensconced on a small island—our first stop before ultimately landing in New Greece's capital—for the past two hundred years. Whenever the Oracle died, a new one was found—reincarnated into a new body—and installed on the island with remarkable reliability. The fact that most of the time, the reincarnated new Oracle was born before the old Oracle died didn't seem to bother anyone, but that's religion for you.

Despite its ubiquity and popularity among the Center Sea nations, Hellenism was nearly absent in the Slave Fields. The slave religion started as hodgepodge of various Hellenistic, Christian, and Hindu beliefs the scholars of the Library called Kalkaism. Over time, the pantheon of anthropomorphic deities were replaced by a lone messianic figure, promised to free the sentients from their bondage, and you didn't have to be a genius to figure out who was putting herself into that role. If she could pull off a coup for an independent free nation for the former slaves, who's to say she wasn't deserving of a little reverence. Not me, for sure.

I continued reading for the next few hours about the two

religions, focusing on their codified speech, gestures, postures, rituals, dress, and behaviors—anything that would help me blend in once we got to the Oracle's island. It was unlikely I'd be first—it wasn't like I was going to jump to the front of the line—so I would probably have someone to mimic. But if I didn't have that luxury, I would like to pass as a recent wealthy convert, someone that clearly belonged there even if I wasn't fully indoctrinated in the ways of the faith.

At lunch, the cafeteria was abuzz with news of the envoy's arrival and subsequent procession into the depths of the Library. I milled about, soaking in the various versions of events while I ate. The rumor of the envoy had piqued the campus's curiosity, but the general mood matched that of the guardians' dorm; the initial fear on the rebellion's onset had moved to the back burner as the general consensus was that the Library was at little real risk. Classes and research resumed, and no one seemed too bothered as long as their studies and meals were not disturbed. While everyone seemed comforted by the Library's advanced technology, I knew that the Librarian's reliance on technology was a weakness—not a strength—when confronted by an AI. I can't imagine Cara *not* wanting control of the Library if she could finagle it.

I returned to the library after lunch, more out of habit than desire. I had managed to increase my input speed with practice and had scoffed up more than 3,000 different books and corresponding maps, but it was still just a drop in the sea of knowledge that remained unexplored. As I opened the first book of the afternoon—*Circuitry of Dinofini Combat Chassis*—the weight of all the books I would have to leave unread hit me all at once. What was the point? Read one more book, read a hundred more books...I was leaving on a ship tomorrow. Every academic has hit that wall at one point or another: if I can't cram it all in my head before I need it, I might as well piss off and have some fun on my last day.

My mind wandered to the Library's entertainment for the guardians, not the battle chamber but the audio/visual building. With any luck, they'd be showing blissfully brainless and stupid movies, something I could veg out in front of. Mmm...maybe they'd have popcorn? *Screw it—I'm going to the movies!*

I closed my last book and exited the library for a final time. On my way out, I bade the two Grynartis 201A police-patrol robots a salubrious "May you always be lubricated!" and waved goodbye. They ignored me.

I got to Ali Hall just in time to take a seat for a comedic double feature. The first one was about talking dogs saving the day against evil cats while the second was a crazy Thanksgiving Day flick where one of the actors played six different roles. And they did have popcorn, so I stuffed myself full of buttery goodness before returning to my room, a late dinner, and a contemplative coffee while watching the sun descend to the horizon. As it finally crossed the threshold, I toasted it with my coffee, "Here's to an easier trip than last time!"

Chapter Eleven

A New Dawn

Early the next morning, after exercise and a heavy breakfast, I donned the robe and cloak that would cover me for the next three days. The weight and warmth of the wool imbued a sense of gravitas to our upcoming travels that was absent when we were merely trying them on for fit. My breath billowed in the late October air as I waited outside Balfour Hall for Zew and Diana. The air had a bite and I had to fidget to stay warm. Despite the Center Sea's tempering, there was only so much it could moderate the dramatic temperature swings common to the old Great Plains.

As we walked to the Chimera Gate, our new clothing attracted everyone's attention, but they'd always look away after giving us the once over. By adopting pilgrim garments, we were simultaneously broadcasting our presence while removing our unique identifiers. I felt like a red and white chameleon—everyone would see us but no one would really know it was us under the garb. We would conspicuously blend into the background. Clearly, the power of uniforms hadn't changed beneath the shattered moon.

We passed through the gates and into the southern enclosure where sentients were up and preparing for the long day ahead even though the sun was still below the horizon. Unlike the northern enclosure, which was filled with vehicles gearing up for one of the final returns to Las Vegas this year, the southern enclosure was entirely non-mechanical. Filled with horses, donkeys, camels, and a few shattered moon beasts of burden, the smell of exhaust and gas was replaced by the odor of dung and the snuffle and grumble of living creatures.

Armed with my research in the Library, I took note of the native animals. I recognized the ever-popular turzard—a combination turtle and lizard with a poisonous spit—from my time in Vegas, but the multi-legged horse with compound eyes was new to me. Called an equipede, they were favored draft animals in rocky terrain. I even spotted a pair of telepanths, giant telepathic panthers, which I assumed were steeds for wealthy guards as they would never deign themselves to be used as baggage carriers.

Our original plan, back when we were going to travel to the Great Sumi under the ZZZ's contact, was to purchase or hire some horses and ride our way to the coast. However, there wasn't any chance of that happening now with the fighting, and we walked out of the southern enclosure toward the rising sun. Limon was about ten miles away and we'd be there in a few hours if our luck held. To dissuade marauders, we each carried thick walking sticks that could properly be described as staffs since it was taboo for pilgrims to openly carry weapons. Although I was lacking in the beard department, I felt a bit like a mythological wizard as I trudged beside the road, a muddy mess from yesterday's rain.

Soldiers raced past us heading in both directions, and we quickly learned there was fighting no more than four miles away. So much for the campus rumor of an eight-mile safety zone! As we went, we kept our heads down and eyes open, walking single-file—Zew in front, Diana in the middle, and then myself bringing up the rear. We'd agreed that Zew would do all the talking for us as his Greek was impeccable; that would help maintain our cover if we needed to convince anyone that we were really Hellenes on a pilgrimage. Not only did that help our cover as pilgrims, but it also reduced our chances of death by former slaves—New Greece had no stake in the Slave Fields of Colorado, so the slaves would be more inclined to treat us fairly.

The rising sun turned the moisture into mist and then into a full-blown fog. After a half mile, the road narrowed and the terrain roughened, filling up with trees. We opted for the edge of the muddy road rather than walking next to it in the fog. I hated walking in the mud, as does any sane sentient, but it was better than losing one's footing. The drudgery of repetitive sucking steps became the soundtrack of our journey to the port.

Eventually, the sun burned off the fog to reveal a clear crisp day, punctuated with occasional musket fire from the east. We kept at the road until we came upon the rear of a Library unit that demanded our identification. A brief discussion cleared up where we'd come from and where we were going.

"I'll let you by, but I'd pick next year to make your pilgrimage, if I were you," the corporal advised us. "The Oracle's still going to be there."

"We'd like to," Zew explained, touching Diana's shoulder, "but we've already been childless for too long and we can't abide it any longer. It may be our last chance." Diana took the lie in stride so well, I wondered if they'd discussed it previously.

"I understand; I'm just saying you gotta be alive if you want to have children, you know?" The corporal replied earnestly. "Those slave bastards aren't going to treat you well."

"We'll have to trust Soteria to protect us," Zew responded piously, his deliberately thickened Greek accent selling the tale. "We just can't wait anymore." The corporal nodded and waved us through, leaving us between enemy forces.

"I wish I believed in Soteria," I muttered once we were out of earshot, "'cause here comes the tricky part."

"I'm right with you on that one," Diana agreed. "Let's hope the plan works, but be ready to draw that blaster of yours."

A few moments later, we crested a small hill and the trees parted, revealing the full measure of destruction that war places upon the land and those that live on it. There were bodies everywhere as far as we could see: bodies upon the ground, bodies among the once-green mounds, bodies in smoldering patches of grass, bodies on the shores of the small river running toward the Center Sea, bodies in the trees, and bodies in the burnt ashes of the village to our south.

The road was the only geography spared the flesh of the dead—they had been dragged off of it and piled either to the side of the road or in front of the hastily erected barricade that stood before us. Several dozen glaring sentients manned the structure, deciding if we should live or die based on our appearance and whether or not they thought we believed them property and therefore not free. I have been in many dangerous places and I've taken many risks, but I don't think any have been greater than that half mile walk down the middle of a bloody road straight into the arms of a desperate army.

We walked slower than normal down the hill, exaggerating our movements to emphasize that we carried wooden staffs, *not* firearms. A tense three minutes passed until we were hailed by the slave commander.

"Halt!" a voice cried out. It came from a tough-looking moose sentient carrying a rifle with the unmistakable silhouette of an AK-47. We stopped, holding our arms out to our sides, and she and a half dozen other sentients approached us. They were a ragged bunch, several of which were malnourished, but as they neared, I could see the fire in their eyes didn't match the emptiness of their bellies. They drew closer, weapons pointed at us, and the moose yelled again, "Identify yourself!"

"Do you speak Greek?" Zew responded in Greek.

"Yes, I do. Identify you!" the moose sentient replied in broken Greek.

"I am Zoilus and this is my deaf wife, Diana. We are seeking the Oracle's help to provide us children. This other is Petrinos, our cousin, who seeks a cure for his impotence. We traveled to the Library for their knowledge, but they were unable to help us, so we are going to beseech Hera."

Zew's speech calmed the moose sentient. She translated what he'd said to her fellow soldiers and they relaxed as well.

"It is good thing you do. Pass yes. Money need. Or food," she garbled out sternly.

Zew nodded and ordered, "Petrinos, pay each of these guards a lady and give them your rations for today. We will eat tomorrow." As I did as commanded, he feigned a sign-language communiqué with Diana, who handed over her rations as Zew did his. The soldiers waved us by as they dug into our foodstuffs and distributed the ladies.

Now that we were in "enemy" territory, we could relax a bit. Cara's information about the treatment of pilgrims seemed accurate and our idea to pretend to be Greek—conveying to the slaves that we didn't own slaves ourselves—had surely helped. To them, we were as we appeared: a third party not involved in the fight. We encountered two more groups before entering Limon, but each let us pass with a small "gift." They all asked for food, but seemed satisfied with our explanation that we'd given all our food to the soldiers on the front.

Limon was in better shape than I thought it would be; I guess the rebellion hit so fast and hard that it didn't have time to put up much of a fight. Our robes were enough to secure us entrance and we passed through the tall stone gatehouse into the city with nary a glance paid to us. We had a few hours before *The Seeker* would cast off at noontide, but the docks were our first stop inside the city, to ensure we wouldn't miss her.

On the way to the docks, I noticed many empty storefronts; only the bakers, blacksmiths, cobblers, and weavers were open. Other than that, everything was closed. When we arrived at the docks, I understood why. While I anticipated there would be a "cleansing" of some sort, I wasn't prepared for the magnitude of reckoning that greeted us when we entered the main square: hundreds of dead bodies had been tossed onto a ship that was preparing to sail. The name on the side of the ship was the *John Kimber*, and if that name meant what I thought it meant, it was apropos that the rebels chose it as the final vessel for those who sided with their previous masters. On deck, there were piles and piles of bodies with open barrels of oil wedged between the mounds of corpses. And although I had no way to know how many dead were in the hold, I took a small comfort that at least the young looked to be spared from the assault—albeit as orphans—from the lack of small youthful bodies on the piles.

Locating *The Seeker* was easy, as the docks were nearly

empty. We met with Duronga the captain, a sentient of mouse heritage, and she showed us about the ship and our quarters—nothing more than three hammocks and a chest to stow our packs, but better than being on deck. The ship was already full of pilgrims, as apparently everyone had the same idea we had—get here early and hunker down.

Once we'd finished arranging everything below deck, Zew maintained our cover with an observation, "The rest of the docks are empty compared to when we arrived."

"Well, look at that," Duronga nodded toward the now-burning *John Kimber*, "and you'll know why."

"Have they been burning all the ships?"

"No, that's the only one so far, but no one else wanted to chance it and they left as soon as they could. I've been coming and going here for a decade, and the slaves would never touch a pilgrimage ship, but everyone else..." She shrugged and let the thought trail away.

"Who's that?" I asked, pointing to a ship on the horizon.

She turned her head out to look and squinted. "Looks like a trireme. That ship would either be from New Greece or Amarillo. I can't quite see the *episema* yet." She pursed her lips in thought. "They're heading our way, so I hope you're done with your business in the city—I'm going to leave dock and drop anchor in the bay to ride out this encounter."

She dismissed us without a word, and the ship soon bustled with yells and activity. As we cruised into deeper water, I kept my eyes on the trireme. Although they would have instantly provided what we needed to know, I decided against pulling out my binoculars; I'd rather no one else on the ship know I'd anything worth stealing. Ten minutes later, we were a good three hundred yards into the bay and a heavy splash heralded the anchor drop.

A stillness came over the ship, like a mouse as the shadow of the hawk falls upon it. Pilgrims and crew alike cautiously watched the trireme oar past us a little less than an hour later. It was a beautiful ship, obviously built for war, and flew the episema of the Island Empire of Amarillo—a solid black alpha turned on its side to look like a bull upon a field of green. Upon its decks were rows of soldiers, at least two hundred in addition to the normal crew of the same number to power such a vessel.

The Greeks beneath the shattered moon fought in pairs: musketeer and shield master. Each soldier bore a musket, and hanging off the trim sides of the *Lysandros* were dozens of large shields with spikes at their bottom and notches on their top right.

While normal shields weren't much defense against musket fire, the Greeks made their shields heavier and thicker as they were an integral part in their style of warfare. Whoever their intended target was, *The Seeker* breathed a collective sigh of relief once the warship sailed past without harassment.

"I wonder what are they up to?" I quietly muttered to Zew

since he seemed to have knowledge of the area; his Greek was flawless.

"Not sure," he responded tersely. "Looks like an invading force, but if so, there would be more ships than just the one."

Suddenly, it dawned on me. "They've made an alliance or bought mercenaries!" I spoke a bit louder than I should have. It caused a stir among the other pilgrims, and they all lingered with us on deck until the *Lysandros* docked in Limon, greeted with friendship.

"He was right!" one of the pilgrims said, awed.

"How did he know?" another asked.

"It was just a guess," I explained. "It had to be something like that, or the city would have been in an uproar upon their approach." That seemed to satisfy them and they went back to ignoring me, which was where I felt most comfortable.

Apparently, Cara had made some deals. Depending on the scope of them, things could get very ugly for the Boneyard and the Library. If she'd offered up the entire port—or even just dropped the customary docking fees and tax assessments—to Amarillo in exchange for support in the war, there was little chance she'd lose. It was one thing to have two thousand armed slaves and quite another to have a highly trained military force of two hundred that carried shields capable of stopping return fire. Their presence could turn the tide in the Boneyard and the Library toward settlement and the creation of a new, non-slave nation state. And what if this was just the first of several shiploads of soldiers?

I wanted to tell someone about the whole beautiful strategy, but the only sentient I could say anything to was off somewhere leading a revolution. I had to be content with watching the soldiers disembark with a big grin on my face.

"You seem inordinately happy," Diana noted my odd shift in demeanor.

I shrugged. "Can't a pilgrim be excited to embark for New Pythia?"

Chapter Twelve

Miles Before I Sleep

We set sail with the prevailing wind when the tide came in, allowing *The Seeker* to easily pass over the shallows at the mouth of the bay and into the main mass of the giant body of water. The vessel was a sort of modified carrack, smaller than normal, and it would be dubious to call it ocean-worthy in its current state, but it was enough to deal with the swells of the Center Sea.

The wind was strong and the sails taut as we tacked starboard toward the southeast. We had a hundred or so nautical miles to go until New Pythia—more commonly called the Isle of the Oracle—and we wouldn't see it until tomorrow evening, even if we kept up the near-maximum speed provided by the favorable wind because *The Seeker* was filled to the gills with pilgrims and running low in the water. Given the general lack of religiousness among our traveling companions, I suspected we weren't the only bunch more focused on leaving the Library than seeking the Oracle's wisdom.

While I was glad Cara arranged us safe passage out of the Library before starting a revolution, she did fail to mention the downside of posing as sojourners, something I only found out after researching in the stacks. One of the requirements specific to visiting the Oracle is that pilgrims can't sleep once they're on the waters of the Center Sea. The hammocks we were assigned weren't for sleeping, they were a place to get us out from underfoot of the crew and to retreat to in case of bad weather. We could rest in the hammocks, but sleeping was strictly verboten. We had a long taxing trip ahead of us.

Since the weather was nice, I eschewed the dark creaking quarters below desk and copped a squat along the edge of the forecastle, dangling my legs through the railing slats and over the side. I'd spent most of last month indoors under the variable lighting of a Granger follow lamp and missed all the bright sunny days of early autumn. The sea air was brisk and chilly, but clean and crisp with nary the hint of vanilla that dominates the air of all book repositories.

A variety of birds crowded the sky, most of them typical to the area in and around the Great Lakes this time of year, but there were a few surprises. A swoon of kittiwakes dove by the ship minutes after I sat down, and large numbers of Hudsonian godwits were traveling in all directions. Given their ubiquity, the godwits must have claimed the Central Sea as a new winter home. In my time, they underwent a giant migration; they should have been somewhere south of the border this late in autumn. At some point during my sea-sprayed reverie, a little cartoon popped into my head featuring a tired godwit flopping down on the shores of the Center Sea with a speech bubble proclaiming, "Forget South America—this is good enough!"

It was enough to tip me into a chortle and startle the other sentients on deck, but I couldn't care less. The water and wind was stripping away tensions I'd carried since arriving in Las Vegas, and I wasn't going to let social convention get in the way of my revitalization. After the past couple of months, I needed a good laugh.

It didn't take long until the land was lost to view. We skimmed along waves of blue mirroring clear azure skies. Once we were encased in that singular color, other ships started appearing. None of them drew very close and none of them were heading toward the west coast, but their sheer volume was impressive nonetheless. We rarely spent any time alone on the water, and the ship traffic only increased the farther east we went. All of them were sailing vessels; many were also oared like the *Lysandros* that passed us earlier.

I had yet to see any motorized vessels and hoped to catch sight of one in the water, as it was unlikely I would get the chance once we entered port in Naxos. I imagined motored ships would be kept back for martial purposes—no need to burn oil to do some fishing or shipping. The rub was that Naxos had a separate walled military harbor, so once *The Seeker* docked, I would either have to sneak in to get a look or snag an invite to the imperial palace; that was the only part of the city that overlooked the military harbor.

As the temperature rose with the midday sun, the wind on the open water picked up and I surrendered my vantage spot to an eager-looking youth. There were only a few younger sentients or children among the pilgrims; most were full adults and many were on the downward slope of life. I went below deck to grab a few slices of bread and a hunk of cheese that came with passage and filled a wooden cup with freshly harvested water. As a freshwater sea, drinking water was easy to come by; one of the crewmembers continually dipped a large funnel-like oar into the passing waves, pulling it up and allowing it to drain into a small barrel that was sealed and then rolled down to the mess. It was one of those clever low-tech-beneath-the-shattered-moon solutions that pleased the logistical manager in me.

I elbowed a space at the crowded table and dove into my simple meal with gusto. The conversations around me were banal, but comforting. It had been a long time since I was surrounded by "normal" sentients and I enjoyed their presence in a way I hadn't since leaving Deeplac. The inhabitants of Las Vegas had that unequivocal indifference characteristic of crowded cities and you can imagine the kind of conversations I had endured shuttered in with cloistered academics. I was finally moving after weeks of stagnation, and I started to feel more like the clean water in my cup than the brackish pool I had become under the Granger lamp in the stacks.

After the meal, I found a spot along the starboard side of

the ship and watched the sun slowly arc its way toward the horizon for a few hours before a wall of clouds rolled in from the north, tinting and muting the living canvas. The wind turned cold, the barometric pressure dropped, and the rain followed a few minutes after sunset. Those fortunate enough to have an assigned space below deck made for our hammocks. When the sun was away, the hold was illuminated by half a dozen oil lamps that danced with the rolling of the ship. Each hammock had a flap of cloth with a stout string at the end, and I climbed in and secured myself with a bow knot.

I tried to ride that fine line between relaxation and sleep, but the dim lighting, swaying of the ship, and white noise of the patter of the rain threatened to lull me to sleep. Luckily, there were pilgrims onboard who'd taken it upon themselves to walk through the berth and shake sentients to ensure the ways of the Oracle were minded; no one would sleep for very long under their pious watchful eyes.

The evening passed and morning dawned a cloudy, windy day. After a night crammed below, I opted to take my bread on deck and enjoy breakfast al fresco. The sea had roughened and more than a few of the passengers gifted the waters the nutrients of their bellies to the snickers and smiles of the crew. Thankfully, I wasn't prone to either motion sickness or fear of heights; not that the two were medically related, but looking up at three of the sailors in the rigging coupled them in my mind at the moment. They set the sails to the shifting winds high above the deck as *The Seeker* skipped across the choppy waves.

We had most of the day to go before the Isle of the Oracle would be visible to those of us on deck. I claimed a place near the bowsprit that was out of the way of the crew and chewed on the now-stale bread; it wasn't much, but it was something. There would be time enough for food; for now, forward movement on the waves and through the wind was nourishment enough. The thick woolen robe and cloak did much to cut down the chill, but after a few hours out in the open, I headed below deck once again to warm up. Wrapped and tied in my hammock, I spent my final hours in a state of near sleep, being constantly jarred by monitoring pilgrims.

The long-awaited cry of land brought everyone back to their senses as *The Seeker* turned toward the west. Zew, Diana, and I had decided to be at the end of the line, so we left our equipment in place as others gathered theirs and headed above deck. Finally, we slowly slid into port and all movement stopped. We donned our packs and disembarked the ship.

New Pythia was a rocky island, nearly vertical, densely populated, and it wouldn't surprise me to find that most of the inhabitants were associated with the numerous temples and their associated pilgrimages. Wooden docks sprawled across the water and converged into the city's stone-walled extents. This late in the season, there were only eight other ships in the small port, which could accommodate dozens similarly sized to *The*

Seeker.

We followed the line of pilgrims heading up the slopes into the depths of the town. The construction was purely Greek—stone, rectangular, tiled, polychrome—and the ornamentation was almost entirely Doric, although a few temples were faced with Ionian columns. We trudged up step after step, a single red line of crimson cloaks, until finally arriving at the peak of the acropolis. Atypical of the traditional Greek city, the acropolis was solely populated by temples and dominated by the massive circular Temple of the Oracle, the only building of that shape I'd seen in the entire city. Unlike the other buildings, it had ornate columns of an order I didn't recognize. Perhaps they were unique to the Oracle, but I couldn't be sure as I hadn't studied any texts on New Greek architecture.

Our column ground to a halt once the first of us entered the temple, but after a few minutes we were all corralled inside. The temple was unlike any other Greek temples I'd read about; it was mostly empty, except for a small internal room that was more like a miniature theater than a religious place. Along one side of the room were rows of seats carved into the very rock of the acropolis, barely enough to accommodate our hundred strong. Opposite that was a stage upon which a lone cauldron boiled. The inside was lit by dimly flickering torches and the gleaming charcoal under the heated pot drew your eye to the stage—enigmatic lighting to set the mood. I reconsidered my initial assessment: perhaps all religion *was* more theater than anyone would like to admit.

We took our cushioned seats on the rock-carved chamber and as soon as we'd all settled, music started emanating from behind the stage façade: a stylized imaged of the ideal Greek city. The cadence was ragged and the tones dissonant; the rhythm was jangly, like barely controlled chaos. The air filled with powerful drumbeats and staccato movements—primitive, raw, and uniquely Greek. If I ever made it back to my timeline or anything close to it, I'd love to transfer my recording of it to a Greek scholar just to watch their eyes light up—I was experiencing a history they could only read about.

Even though I considered myself anesthetized to such devices, the music brought me into the place and time, singularly focused on the task at hand, so much so that when the music suddenly ended in a resounding crescendo, I was entirely fixated in the moment.

And then the Oracle entered.

Chapter Thirteen

Truths Revealed

The Oracle was a nude preteen boy with a shock of stringy black hair. He looked to be completely human and was thin, wild, and dirty. A golden collar encircled his neck, attached by golden chains to two other golden collars around the necks of two nude adult sentients: one of an undeterminable mammalian background and the other reptilian. Both of them had their eyes gouged out, and the Oracle dragged them behind him as he scampered to the boiling cauldron. As he approached, the water flashed with a smoky bang and luminous purple flames rose out over the rim, taking shape into unique faces and bodies before quickly roiling away into new visages and forms.

"I am the Oracle!" the young boy yelled in a shrill and girlish voice, still many years short of puberty's change. "I am and will be and when you are dust, I will remain!" The flames cast an amethyst glow across his leering countenance: eyes narrowed, mouth ajar, and tongue lolling at the pilgrims who'd come to seek his blessings or predictions. He danced back and forth on stage, pulling his blind and chained sentients with him as he went.

Suddenly he stopped and howled, baring his blackened teeth before pointing in my general direction. "You! How *dare* you return! I have given you your future and you did not take it. Now you suffer under what I have laid upon you and yet you return? You return?!" Everyone in the crowd turned to look, not at me but Zew, who was sitting next to me and who had removed his cloak, exposing his chiseled face and upright, multicolored mohawk.

"Zoilus Zelos, son and last remaining member of House Zelos, you defied your fate twenty and one hundred years ago! You have no future, you have no past, you are damned to walk the earth until you cease taking lives, until you cease to defy me and marry a daughter of House Nike. You are outcast! Begone now! There are others here whose fates are still open. Yours is a tomb. Begone!"

The crowd's reaction couldn't have been more electric if an actual bolt of lightning had thundered down upon the ageless noble of New Greece. Gasps and cries reverberated throughout the temple. Before them stood a member of a house declared dead no more than a decade ago by the empress—a house shorn of all its possessions and once second in power only to the royal house itself. The consequences of a claimant to the Zelos fortune would shake the foundations of the state, and none could dare challenge the claim as it was the Oracle himself who made it.

Zew rose and slowly walked out of the temple, indifferent to the stares of the pilgrims and the magical roiling purple fire over the cauldron. Before he exited, he turned to the Oracle and declared, "I am no pawn and my future is my own. One I will make with my own hands." I now understood his demeanor completely—I'd mistaken it for that of a survivalist, a loner, a barbarian...but he was a noble, raised in privilege and obligation. His recalcitrance was one of superiority, not hesitance or caution.

Diana rose to follow Zew, indifferent to the Oracle, but she was called next by the cavorting seer. "Blade Witch, you think you escape your future by leaving? Your flesh will never bleed from the edge's touch, but beware the blades of the heart!" The scrawny youth cackled at what he saw in the turbulent flames, refusing to elucidate the cryptic words or fiery images he saw. Diana paused while he spoke and let his laughter die off before replying with a short dismissive sneer, not unlike what I imagined she would deliver to a petulant teenage boy making advances at her. She exited the temple without a backward glance.

This incensed the Oracle, who started wailing and tearing at his hair. The blinded sentients chained to him groaned as well, like unwilling extensions of his will. The flames changed from purple to green, and the bodies and faces within them changed from fleshy to skeletal.

"And you!" The Oracle burst his anger upon me with

another pointed finger. "You, companion of the cursed and the proud! Your fate is sealed by your desires—every family you make will crumble as did your first, and the death that follows you is a grand vulture feeding off the scraps of your table until you finally surrender. None of what you do will last and your new name will be forgotten, just as your old one."

Whatever, you stinking sorcerous little brat—I'm not the one naked and covered in dirt. I got up and followed Diana and Zew. No point in trying to lay low after this debacle. I squashed my desire to flip off the Oracle when I left and was surprised to find it was now night outside. *What the...?* My internal clock said it was only 3:25 p.m., and last time I checked with reality, that's well before night. Zew and Diana were standing in the center of the massive courtyard of the acropolis.

I interrupted their conversation. "What the hell time is it?"

"A bit past midnight," Zew answered. "It's always midnight when the first sentient leaves the Oracle."

Stupid magic. I reset my clock. "Well, that was exciting!" I exclaimed with a big ass grin on my face. "I can't wait to see your palaces, noble Zoilus."

"That's not funny, Stonewall," Diana retorted.

"Really? Because it seems hilarious to me right now. I'm sure I'll feel differently in the morning, but hey, who knows who's going to know we're heading to the capital by tomorrow. Maybe they'll have a grand audience ready and we can get some palanquins so we don't have to walk everywhere?"

"I didn't expect him to remember—" Zew replied tersely.

"Obviously."

"...and I didn't expect him to be such a little bastard about it, either."

"He's used to getting his way." I shrugged. "Powerful people get real prickly when others don't obey them like they're supposed to."

"Look, Stonewall, I get that you're upset, but right now we've got to come up with a plan to get us to the other side of the sea with minimal disturbance," Zew growled back in frustration.

"Okay, sure." I didn't like where this was headed. "Any *other* reason why we can't stick to our old plan?"

Zew rubbed his mohawk and sighed. "Long story made short, not only am I the last living noble of House Zelos...I've also garnered a reputation as being the Pirate King Corrigan, which is a lot more recent and the reason why I washed up on Deeplac's shore. I was defeated by New Greece's imperial navy and fled through the wasteland before arriving there. There aren't a lot of people in Naxos who would recognize me as Corrigan, but if they do because of all the commotion that will be caused by the Oracle identifying me as Zoilus, we're in for a tough time."

That washed over me like a giant wave of "literally, what the hell, man?!" and then I started giggling. "Cursed immortal Greek noble descended from the gods, dread pirate king—

what are you, a living Gilbert and Sullivan character? No, wait, Alexander Dumas would suit you better!" Both of them stared at me, but I just kept laughing, the absurdity not helped by my sleep deprivation.

"He's not going to be much help right now," Diana concluded—which made me laugh harder. Yeah, I wasn't going to be much help; I was going to solve the problem. Who needs help when you know a fixer?

"This is not that hard to mend. First, you keep your head uncovered at all times from here on out. Show them that you're not afraid to be recognized," I ordered Zew. "Demand their attention. Be the noble you are. When we finally get to Naxos, it's going to be night. We immediately drop the pilgrim garb, shave off that ridiculous hair of yours, break into a local theater, steal their makeup, and then I'll do you over so that no one will recognize you. You'll be a ghost. Everyone will be looking for you, everyone will know you're there, but no one will find you. And then we find a ship heading out to Great Suomi as quickly as we can and get the hell out of Dodge. No reasonable sentient would expect the newly returned heir of a noble house to behave like that—it's going to be easy."

They both smiled at me. "Sometimes it's nice to have someone as naturally devious as you around," Zew complimented me.

"Sometimes," Diana qualified.

"Let's get moving," Zew suggested. "Normally no one

leaves until the Oracle's done with everyone, but today may be different. I'd like to get back on the ship before word gets out."

Chapter Fourteen

Suck Ups and Sycophants

We returned early to *The Seeker* to the surprise of the captain; it was customary for all sojourners to spend the night at the pilgrim barracks to catch some much-needed sleep before sailing out an hour before noon. However, Zew talked her into letting us stay on the ship with the help of an eagle. Neither the captain nor the crew knew Zew's true identity, unlike everyone that would be bunking in the barracks tonight, and we really needed to sleep. Although he was supposed to make his presence known for the initial part of our plan, that could wait until tomorrow when the other pilgrims returned to the ship.

"This is what's going to happen," Zew spoke softly once we had some privacy below decks. "The reason why I wanted to come here instead of the barracks is that almost all of the pilgrims who come to the Oracle are wealthy, politically-connected sentients who wouldn't waste a moment of time before introducing themselves to me, a powerful new player in their great game."

That made a lot of sense to me. Hell, I wouldn't be surprised if some of them tried to get onto the ship once they realized Zew wasn't in the barracks. They might even go as far as attempting to bribe Duronga as we did, although I doubt it would be welcomed—with over ninety sentients waiting to receive the Oracle's visions, it would be well into the night before they would even be able to check the barracks and disturbing the sleep of the crew that late would elicit more than a few curses and yells—they needed the sleep just as badly as we did.

Zew continued, "If you two are amenable to the idea, I propose to set you up as gatekeepers." He turned his eyes to Diana. "You'll be my personal guard, as you're not smarmy enough to be my majordomo."

"Unlike me," I chimed in with a little bow.

"Precisely. With all the information you've crammed into your head after weeks in the library and with your passable Greek, you're well primed to filter contacts to keep up appearances of my return." I was about to defend my Greek, but Zew was on a roll. "Putting you in charge of the meet and greet should make it easier for you to see any new threats or modify your plan as needed. Make any promises you think necessary and remember everyone that comes to you and everything that's said or implied.

"Once the throng returns in the morning, Duronga will learn of my true lineage and decide to move us to her quarters, which we'll gladly accept, along with the rights of first exit once we dock at Naxos. She may even try to return our bribe but don't accept it—if we refuse the return, she'll feel obligated to help us if we need any additional assistance in the future. She'll worry about owning me a debt."

The last time Zew had said this much in one stretch, he was discussing the ins and outs of eating different kinds of sausages. Behind the muscles, discipline, and taciturnity, there was a brain seeped in political acumen. That was nice to know, doubly so because it was probably killing him to reveal this much about himself.

With our initial plan fleshed out, we grabbed some shuteye. I slept in a hammock nearest the entrance while Diana and Zew slept in a pair farthest away. I managed to grab a solid five hours before the first of the returning pilgrims started making noises on the docks. The crew ignored them for a good half hour and we joined them for a meager breakfast of beans and stale bread. They were an all-right bunch—enjoyed a good crude joke like all sailors the world over. I felt a bit sorry for them once they learned that Zew was a noble.

The New Greeks—unlike the ancient Greeks—didn't have slaves, which I took as an admirable change, but they did have an extremely inequitable social and legal system. Just being convivial with one above your station could land you in hot water, but treating a noble like a common crewmember? That could get you lashes or even death if the noble pressed the issue. The standards were relaxed during religious pilgrimages, as it was expected that all strata would be forced to comingle, but even then status and standing were always present. I could see the near physical distress the guards experienced when they became aware of Zew's status change and remembered of how they'd behaved around and with him.

Everything went down as Zew predicted, and soon we were ensconced in the captain's quarters for privacy. It wasn't long before I was approached by multiple newcomers; as they arrived, I triaged their appeals according to standing and importance. By the time we set sail, there was an impromptu line stretching into the berths.

I spent the first hour arranging the order of the meetings. Once that was established, I proceeded to escort each petitioner into the captain's quarters and listen to the exchange. Many of the guests were surprised that neither Zew nor I wrote anything down, but most were too nervous to ask. A few of higher station did, to which Zew's response of, "My majordomo never forgets a name, a face, nor a conversation," amply satisfied their curiosity as well as conveyed a not-too-subtle threat.

The reasons for meeting with him ranged from simple invitations all the way to marriage propositions. Some of the petitioners were rather pushy, but none continued pressing their luck once Diana emphasized her presence, triggered by a hand signal from Zew. While she was personally beneath their station, in her capacity as guardian of Zoilus Zelos, she acted with his authority. It didn't take more than a well-timed cough from her to send them scurrying. I was just the mouthpiece, she was the weapon of war.

The trip to Naxos took ten hours and except for an hour in which we took a meal, Zew saw a constant stream of visitors. The relentlessness of the applicants gave me a bit of insight into why Zew didn't want anyone to know his pedigree. Although he seemed unfazed by the onslaught, I'd been with him long enough to notice the small tells in his body language that indicated he was already tired of the process. He may have been born into his status, but he wasn't born *for* it.

Diana fared worse than he did. She was a sentient of action, and guarding someone who didn't need help protecting himself while listening to dozens of conversations in a language she didn't understand got to her quickly. By the end of the day, I knew what her personal hell would look like.

When I closed the door on the final pilgrim, they let out a simultaneous sigh of relief. I left them alone to recuperate from the social onslaught and asked the captain for our current time, walking back leisurely before reporting, "We've got about an hour till we dock."

"Good," Diana replied. "Which of the theaters would be the best to hit?"

"If everything's the way it was when I was last there a decade ago, the Polykleitos would be my first choice, with the Aspasia a close second. The Polykleitos is the larger of the two." Zew stroked his chin, thinking. "But the new theater I was invited to attend by one of the pilgrims, the Pelasgian, could be an option. Since it's new, small, and in the round, it may have the weakest security."

"Let's go to the closest first and check it out. If it appears well guarded, we'll move on to the next. If they all appear equally guarded, we'll go with the last of them," I suggested.

"That'd be the Pelasgian. It's just off the docks."

We gathered our belongings and spent our final minutes on board watching the approach of the city. The rest of *The Seeker's* passengers gave us wide berth and ingratiating bows as we gazed at the full moon in the cloudless night, the torches and lamps of the city glimmering in the water. Naxos straddled the flat isthmus between the rising lobes of Kandelioussa, the largest island of Thalassocracy of New Greece. It was close to the size of the ancient Peloponnese and shaped much like a reverse saddle, with the ends of the island curving upward and the center gently sloped.

Outside the city's towering white walls, the lands were sparsely inhabited and mostly sectioned off into large farming cooperatives. Each plot was partitioned into shares owned by many prominent families, tying many individuals into the success or failure of any one farm. Such an arrangement acted as a hedge for any one family but also promoted social cohesion through economic interdependence. Share trading in the farming cooperatives—both on the main island and on other islands—was a common sort of political activity and on a whim, I discreetly asked Zew if he owned any.

"Not technically. Since House Zelos was broken up, the lands were divested into many different hands...but since the divestitures were illegal, my ownership would be uncontested once I established who I am. Were that the case, I'd own most of the land south of Naxos."

"I can see why your arrival is causing such a stir," I replied. The land alone would be worth millions of eagles, not to mention the products made from it, all of which were easily transported and sold to the nearby large populace.

"And that's why we'll need to watch out for assassins," he added. "There are many who won't welcome my return, who believe that I'll impoverish them, who won't think twice about taking care of their problem directly."

I smiled. "That's why I'm your majordomo—assassins were the first thing that crossed my mind."

Diana nodded. "Mine as well." She might not be an ex-assassin, but she had a higher stake in his wellbeing than I did, so it wasn't surprising her mind ran the same train of thought as mine on this occasion.

As *The Seeker* docked, I was heartened to find that the New Greeks didn't have the same policy of weapon confiscation and item taxation as the Lucky Duchy. All they had to receive us was a pair of sentients who took down our names and from which ship we'd departed. We'd convinced the captain to hold the other pilgrims on the ship until we were off the docks—Duke Zelos would like some privacy during his magnificent return to his homeland—and she gladly let us depart first.

Zew went before us, and his calm statement, "Duke Zoilus Zelos, last member of House Zelos," made the bored guards jump like a cat before a cucumber.

"Pardon, my lord, we did not recognize you," the one with the pen stammered with a bow.

"You will. Everyone will."

I'll give him this, he does scary well...and with a purpose—the guards were so rattled that Diana and I entered the city only listed as "and servants," ensuring us some anonymity. After being checked in, we walked down the long wooden pier used for night docking, our boots leaving marks on the softly sanded surface. Halfway down, we were passed by the second guard, sprinting toward the city.

"There goes the news," Zew capitulated. "He's bound for the palace, or I'm a horc."

"Once we're off the dock and out of sight, we discard our robes and start running," I reminded them. "We should have a good five to ten minutes head start ahead of the news, but after that, I don't know."

They both nodded and as we made the turn, cloaks and robes flew off. We dashed down the long street running parallel to the shore and didn't stop until we were within blocks of Pelasgian, the theater in the round that was the newest rage of Naxos. We slowed our pace and found an empty alley. I pulled out my KM6800 fighting utility knife. "First, we've got to get rid of your mohawk." Zew nodded and I quickly reaped his multicolored coiffure, leaving only multicolored stubble behind.

"Ah, I wondered why it never seemed to change color."

"Been that way since I was born."

"We'll find some dye and take care of that," I replied, dusting the remaining hairs off his pack.

We returned to the main street and calmly walked the remaining blocks to the Pelasgian to find it occupied and engaged in some avant-garde late night production. Some cautious inquiries revealed it wouldn't be over until after midnight, so we marked that theater off our list and made our way to the gem of Naxos theaters, the Polykleitos.

Built entirely of native stone, it was set among a formal public garden in a prominent natural rise and bore the traditional tripartite structure of a Hellenistic theater. Exquisitely designed both for aesthetics as well as acoustics, the Polykleitos must have seated at least fifteen thousand when full. We approached from the side, the three-story stone skene on our right. I paused the group and quickly whispered, "I looks empty, but I'm going to go in alone, okay? I'll be back in less than half an hour. Find something to do, or just take a night stroll, and return here—I'll be waiting."

"We'll be here," Diana confirmed softly before adding, "Good luck."

After they left, I fished out my adaptive ghillie suit and

threw it over me like a poncho. Normally I'd wear the suit properly, but there didn't look to be much in the way of security, so I opted for ease and speed. As soon as I turned it on, I immediately blended into the surrounding terrain except for my legs from the calf down. I figured I could crouch if I needed to directly avoid detection.

I kept to the small hedges that would block my visible feet from at least one direction and made my way. I was surprised to find that there wasn't a back entrance into the skene—the only way in was via the stage. Crouching against the wall, I edged around the front corner and saw a flickering coming from within the stone structure, presumably a light for a guard. From the front, it was magnificently decorated with soaring columns and ornate details which serendipitously made climbing easy. I shimmed up to the second story, my movements careful, deliberate, and silent.

Still crouching, I crept into a corner and turned my head into the shadows, closing my eyes so they could fully adjust to the darkness. I heard the guard's footsteps on the ground floor, moving from one end of the stage to the other before returning to his station in the middle of the skene. I waited until he settled himself again before continuing inward.

The interior was very dark and I cautiously placed one foot in front of the other, testing for any sudden changes in elevation. I got about ten feet in before the darkness became too absolute to see shadows upon shadow. Since I couldn't risk turning on my flashlight, I retreated from the solid darkness and decided to tackle the problem from another angle—headlong. Once outside, I climbed down to the stage, pulled my knife, and crept up on the guard.

He was an old fellow, sitting cross-legged before a lamp, reading a leather-backed book. I couldn't place his heritage, likely mammalian given how hairy he was except for the top of his head, which shined even in his dim light. I'd gotten the knife around him before he knew I was there and cupped one hand over his mouth. I set the back of the knife against his throat—he wouldn't be able to tell the difference and I didn't want to accidentally kill him if he struggled.

Which he immediately did, but he wasn't nearly as strong as I was. "Here's what's going to happen," I spoke calmly. "You're going to take me to a dressing area that has a makeup kit and I'm going to take that with me, leaving an eagle in its place. You can choose to fight me on this—which is a bad idea—or go along with me and earn an eagle for yourself in the process."

I felt him squirm at my offer.
"If that doesn't seem morally right to you, consider I could just kill you and take it anyway. If we do things my way, you'll come out wealthier, the sap I'm stealing the makeup kit from comes out wealthier, and you'll still probably keep your job, considering you were obviously overpowered by some sort of crazy elite ninja in desperate need of a makeover."

The wriggling stopped.

"We're good? You're agreeing with me that we do this quiet-like and nobody gets hurt?"

He slowly nodded.

"Excellent!" I released him, stepped back, and lit up my flashlight. "Show me the way."

The guard rubbed his neck as he stood up. He tried but failed to hide his shock when he turned around to face his assailant—standing a few feet away from an adaptive ghillie suit is discombobulating. Your eyes say nothing is there but your brain *knows* something is. He relaxed a bit once I stood fully erect and waved my hands out from under my suit; now I was just an indistinct blur with legs and hands, albeit one bearing a knife.

"I'm just a normal guy," I reassured him. "You won't be able to identify me to anyone, so no need to try. Lead the way."

He started moving this time and led me into the skene and downstairs. Despite my preference to stay hidden and do things the stealthy way, I had to admit this was a better option—downstairs would have been my last choice and I could have bumbled around for a lot longer than thirty minutes. We entered a changing room and he pointed at one of the makeup kits, a leather container the size of a large briefcase. I grabbed it, put an eagle on the counter, and delivered up another to him, which he took with a trembling hand.

"You're nuts," the old sentient pronounced after he had the coin in his hand. The bravery of the old shouldn't be underestimated.

"You ain't wrong, pal," I replied before quickly jogging up and out, leaving him to stumble in the dark and giving me a few more minutes head start in case he decided to break our deal.

Chapter Fifteen

Lying Low and Making Hay

The makeup kit was locked, but it was nothing a fast bit of work with my lock picks couldn't fix. Neither of my companions had seen lock picks in action before, and they were amazed by how quickly I could get them to work. I have the feeling they were more of the smash-and-grab type when they encountered a secured payload.

"You can do this to any lock?" Diana inquired curiously.

"Most locks that have a key, yes. Some locks are specifically designed to render these tools useless, but you'd just use other tools on them. No key lock is unpickable with the right materials and enough time."

"How long would it take you to teach me?" she asked.

"If you really want to learn, you could be picking locks within an hour or two. Mastery would depend on how much you practice. And some just have a gift." I bowed slightly in jest, only half-serious in my boast.

Once opened, the kit did the trick, and when we woke up the next morning in a dockside flophouse—we'd rented a private four-bed room—even someone who knew us would be hard pressed to point us out in a crowd. With our disguises applied, I acquired breakfast and brought it back to our room; we'd decided it best that we refrain from being seen with each other as much as possible, so Diana and Zew stayed in. I expected more pushback from the pair on being cooped up, but after the barrage of social interaction on *The Seeker*, I think both warriors had had enough of other sentients for a while.

I relocked the kit and handed the picks to Diana. The sound of metal on metal and her soft cursing bid me farewell as I left our lodgings. The first thing I did was seek out a source of additional makeup; we had a week's worth which should be enough, but I wanted to know where I could get more before we actually needed it. The second thing I did was nose around the docks trying to find a ship to Great Suomi, and as Cara had informed me, trying to find transit to the northern part of the Center Sea this time of the year was proving frustratingly difficult. I traveled throughout the docks all morning, but couldn't find a single ship out.

I returned to our flophouse with some street food and broke the news. "So there's nothing going in that direction. I spoke to individual captains, spoke to the harbormaster's assistant... nothing."

"I could probably pull some strings and *make* something happen," Zew offered between mouths of the spelt bread the Greeks favored. "There are other ports on the island, and some of them are easier to exit than others. I'd have to take off this disguise, however…the sentients I'd need to talk to would need to recognize me."

"This is an island nation—why aren't there more ships?" Diana fumed at the apparent idiocy of it all. "The weather isn't that bad out there!"

"It's the storms. And the pirates," Zew patiently explained. "But mostly the storms. They come in hard and quick during the last months of the year and over time, we've just stopped sending them north for those four or five months."

"So you think you can make contacts in other ports?" I returned to Zew's original point.

"I can, but it'll have to be tonight and I'll need to go alone."

"Well, in that case, I have something that might help." I picked up my pack and dug out the four packets containing the invisibility powder that Cara had given me. "Now's as good as any time to find out how long it works." They gave me quizzical looks as I opened up one of the folded parchment envelopes, exposing the white crystals inside. "Bottom's up!" I toasted jauntily as I poured them into my mouth. They tasted like colors smell, and I must have passed out for a second because the next thing I remembered was waking up on the floor to two panicked warriors.

"It's okay, I'm on the floor, invisible," I mumbled.

"At least give us some warning, Stonewall!" Diana scolded me.

"I didn't know what would happen," I deflected as I stood

up, but the excuse sounded lame even to me.

"Where'd you get it?" Zew grunted.

"A friend of mine gave it to me."

"A friend? What friend? All your friends are here," Diana scoffed.

"Same one that got us the medikit and the ride," I answered tersely. She picked up on my tone.

"Fine. How long are you going to be like that?"

"Don't really know…not too long, however. I have a packet for each of you if you need to really get away. I'll give them to you once I'm back to normal. One word of caution, I wouldn't recommend taking them while on cliff edges or while operating heavy machinery." My joke fell on flat ears, but I soothed myself, believing it would have killed were I in my own time. That's the problem with a lot of my jokes.

"Can you see yourself?" Zew asked.

"Nope. I'm looking right through my body as we speak. Even though the seat is bent under my weight, all I can see are the fibers in the chair. I admit, it's a most unusual feeling…"

"Here," Diana interjected, holding out a piece of spelt bread. "Eat this. I want to see what happens."

We spent the next half hour exploring the whys and wherefores of the invisibility powder. For example, we found out that any item I picked up became invisible, but if I set it down, it became visible again. However, items that were on me when I took the powder remained invisible even when I put them down. We also learned that the powder lasted a little more than an hour. Once I was visible again, I handed them each a packet which they promptly put away for safekeeping.

A few hours later, I was about to go get dinner when someone knocked at the door.

"Who is it?" I called out in Greek.

"The Empress Laconia Argolis IV," a male voice announced.

"Just a second," I immediately responded. I looked at Zew, to the window, and then back at him, silently asking if we should make a break for it.

He shook his head and walked to the door. With his hand on the handle, he whispered to Diana, "It's the empress and her sorcerer, by the sound of it. Please rise when she enters and bow; don't sit and don't speak unless addressed."

We both rose and he opened the door to an old, olive-skinned man who entered, closely followed by a middle-aged woman with solid white eyes. They were wearing naturally colored, plain clothes—he a chiton, she a peplos—and each had wrapped a himation around themselves for extra warmth. Their hair was dark, his cropped close and hers long and held back by a leather clasp.

"Zoilus Zelos," the empress addressed Zew, looking carefully at Diana and me as we bowed, assessing if we posed a threat. If she was surprised by his disguise, I couldn't tell. "You have company."

"Sharp as ever, Laconia," he replied, switching the

conversation into English so Diana could understand. "These are my traveling companions, Diana and Stonewall. Diana, Stonewall—Laconia. The quiet fellow closing the door is Phalinos. He's thoroughly unpleasant and wishing he could turn me into a toad for my impertinence."

"You swore you would not return. You swore you would cause no difficulties," Phalinos bit the words off brusquely. His English was impeccable.

"And I would have, had things not absolutely required it. I'm just passing through—disguised, see?—and will be gone as soon as I can find passage to Great Suomi." Zew's answer changed nothing in the sorcerer's demeanor.

"Calm down, Phalinos. I'm sure grandfather has a reason why he's back in town," Laconia paused dramatically before continuing, "but why on earth he'd visit the Oracle, of all sentients, is beyond even my comprehension."

Grandfather!?

"The war made hell out of my plans and it was either that or sit in a war zone surrounded by desperate slaves until next year. The latter didn't seem congruent with longevity, so I chose this."

"The former may have been a better choice," she pointed out.

"But if I'd done that, I couldn't tell you that Amarillo has made some sort of arrangement with the rebelling slaves—the warship *Lysandros* unloaded two hundred musketeers two days ago." Clever Zew…his arrival would have been the talk of all the pilgrims; which of them would have thought the *Lysandros* was the more-important bit of news when they had such a juicy story to tell about the Oracle and a destroyed House returning from the ashes?

"A full *lochos*?"

"And I would be surprised if there weren't more. We only saw one, but what's the chance only one would be sent if Theotokopoulos is making a land grab? If he could fill the Slave Fields with his soldiers, who would be there to prevent him from taking it all for himself? A bunch of haphazard slaves?"

"And you were going to tell me?" she asked dubiously.

"Tonight, actually. I was going to go out once it was dark. Hiding from sight, remember?"

Her shoulders loosened and she sighed exasperatedly. "I thought you'd decided to go east once the navy took out your little vengeance operation."

"That what you said you'd do when you bargained for your life from the deck of your sinking ship," Phalinos spoke emphatically.

"And it's what I did. I met these two not far from the shores of Lake Michigan, and we would have stayed there if not for finding a high-tech trap that teleported us to Las Vegas. We're simply making our way back east. Nothing more. All we're looking for is a boat out of here." Even though he was telling the truth, there was an ease in his voice and demeanor that

136

really sold it; Zew wouldn't have made a half-bad grifter, if he had the right motivation.

"That's easily accomplished," the empress stated simply. "You'll leave tomorrow via the *Agōgós*. It shouldn't take more than a day to speed you up to Great Suomi and out of my hair. You *will* stay away this time, yes?"

"I swear."

"We've seen how reliable your word is," Phalinos muttered, but a white-eyed stare from Laconia made him look at the floor. "Report to the military harbor gates by nine tomorrow, and you'll be on the water by ten."

Zew nodded. "Thank you."

"And do get rid of that silly makeup. You look like a lizard."

As soon as the door closed behind them, Diana zeroed in on the revelatory surprise in the conversation, "Grandfather?"

"Yes, I'm her grandfather, but only she and a few select others know. It was close to ninety years ago now—a moment of indiscretion."

She snorted and jibbed in a friendly tone, "You've got a lot of secrets, old man."

"Older than the trees," I snarked.

"Older than the hills," she suggested, astutely raising a forefinger.

"As old as the cracked moon?" I rubbed my chin, as if in deep thought.

"Ha ha," Zew answered, the risen corners of his mouth

belying his annoyance. "Joke all you want, but it looks like things have worked out for the best."

Chapter Sixteen

Smooth Sailing and Treachery

The military harbor guard checked for our names, and I felt like I was waiting outside a nightclub, hoping I'd made the guest list as proof that my cover had held up to scrutiny. I couldn't put my finger on why I felt nervous, but my gut was twinging in that peculiar way and I'd been jumpy all night. On the surface, there wasn't any reason to worry: the empress's and our desires were in line and I got the feeling that the sooner we were out of her way, the better for everyone involved. Diana and Zew didn't seem bothered and chalked up my unease to paranoia, but if I've said it once, I'll say it again—just because you're paranoid, doesn't mean someone isn't trying to screw you over. Trust me, I've been the screw enough times to know. They tacitly agreed to be careful and observant on this trip, but I'm pretty sure that was more to get me to shut up than anything else. Hey, I'll take what I can get.

Once we were approved, an escort led us through the jag in the gatehouse and into the harbor that opened up before us. It wasn't a typical ancient Greek harbor and had more resemblance to the cothons of the Phoenician world: a wide single canal nearly parallel with the coast led into a large circular harbor with a docking island in the middle for the largest ships. Seen from the sky, it would look like a sort of watery keyhole in the earth along the coast. Docks ran the length of the canal as well as along the exterior of the circular harbor. Several score of triremes were moored, many in dry dock as winter was the time for inspection and maintenance.

Reserved for the largest warships and valuable motorized vessels, the central island was composed of a single, multi-leveled building—no doubt housing supplies for manning and mooring the advanced ships along its shores. Hulking quinqueremes filled multiple spots, but my attention was drawn to a matching pair of point-class cutters. They were eighty-two-foot patrol boats—metal hulls, diesel engines—that the coast guard used in the mid-to-latter parts of the twentieth century and they were complete with armament. I wouldn't want to be on any oared ship facing down their 20mm autocannons, although I wondered how much ammunition they actually had—such a large caliber had to be scarce under the shattered moon.

Our escort led us into a skiff and rowed us across the water to the central island before passing the boat over to another group heading from whence we came. We walked the circular path on the outside of the central building, dodging the busy workers, sailors, and soldiers engaged in their various tasks until we reached the *Agōgós*, one of the point-class. Empress

Laconia really wanted Zew out of the area if she was using this ship—just the expense in diesel was incredible.

"Here's your reservation, sir." The escort bowed and waited for us to ascend the gangplank before returning to his duties. At the top of plank was another sailor. She was a lean seven-foot-tall sentient of amphibian background, and if the gill slits along her neck were functional, she had no reason to fear the water.

"I'm Captain Eleutherios," she introduced herself. "Welcome to the *Agōgós*, the jewel in the New Greek Fleet. I have been instructed by the empress to take you to the port of Alexandria in Great Suomi. The empress has not informed me of your names or titles; how would you like me to refer to you?"

"I'm Zew, this is Diana, and that's Stonewall. We have no titles of importance."

Eleutherios nodded and started walking the ship. "Our trip should take ten hours. Once we arrive, we'll use the dinghy to transfer to shore." She descended below deck. "Here are your quarters for the trip. It's not much, so feel free to stay on deck if you wish, but please try to remain out from under the feet of the sailors." She left with a perfunctory bow and we settled into the cramped room, three bunks stacked on top of each other and barely eighteen inches wide.

I didn't have any information on the interior of a standard point-cutter, but the quarters looked like an "after-market" modification—they were made out of some crude-looking iron instead of the aluminum and steel that framed the rest of the ship. It wasn't all together surprising; sentients under the shattered moon were industrious at repurposing the materials of the ancients and by all logic, neither the Greeks nor the point-class cutters should be in a freshwater sea in the center of North America. It's only apropos that the New Greeks were pimping their illogical rides.

We left port within the hour, tooling through calm waters under light power. The captain opened her up once we were a few hundred yards from shore and the reassuring rumble of the Cummins engine filled our small compartment. Once underway, we went above deck—we'd spent a lot of time in constrained spaces lately—and enjoyed the sun and wind as we circled a mile off the northern lobe of Kandelioussa before setting a north-northeasterly course toward Alexandria.

Sitting against the bridge behind the massive autocannon, I refreshed my Finnish. It was the language of Great Suomi and although I expected many of the Suomians to also know English, I wasn't counting on it. I'd put my fluency around a B1 on the old CEFR scale, not that it meant anything to anyone anymore. Diana spoke Finnish fluently, hinting at a background that she didn't speak freely about with me. Zew knew a little Finnish, and what little he did speak was very rough, but I'd bet he knew the names of all the different types of Finnish sausage.

We had clear sailing for a few hours, passing island after wooded island. The coasts were littered with small villages and each of the larger islands had at least one major urban area. New Greece was a populated state which had managed to avoid the deforestation and desertification of the Aegean Islands, although I couldn't be certain if it was by accident or design. Either way, it made for exquisite scenery as we powered by them.

The weather held until we lost sight of the northernmost island. Once in the open waters, a cloudbank formed to our southeast and it looked to be a nasty one. One of the sailors informed us that the captain would like us below deck once the weather caught up to us, which it did an hour later. The crests on the Great Lakes could get as high as twenty-eight feet in heavy weather, and I'd no reason to suspect that wasn't the case in the Center Sea. Once the choppy waters swelled into waves, we got out of the way and took cover below.

The weather gradually worsened from rough to terrible, and I could see the rain and wind pummeling the ship through the window in the watertight door leading to our quarters. Flashes of lightning seared through the sky, at first separated by minutes and then seemingly mere seconds. Were it not for our straps, we would have been tossed about the cabin by the relentless waves banging upon starboard side of the *Agōgós*.

After several hours of this pounding, Eleutherios was forced to turn the ship into the waves and winds; the engine surged and calmed as we went up and over the crests. If this storm was typical, I fully understood why the captains of wooden ships surrendered to the season and refused to sail—I couldn't see how a sailing vessel could withstand the beating we were taking.

Just when it seemed the cutter could take no more and we were all rattled to the bone and had considered the prospect of sinking, everything calmed and the sky outside miraculously cleared. Capitalizing on the lull, I dashed out of the cabin and onto the deck. Surrounding us was a giant circular cloud; we were in the eye of what appeared to be a hurricane, although it was unlike any I'd heard of. For starters, hurricanes need massive amounts of warm water to form and the Center Sea provided none. Secondly, they were hundreds of miles in diameter with eyes up to forty miles wide. This eye we were in was barely three miles wide, and that was being generous.

Breaking protocol, I stepped up into the bridge and addressed the captain. "Is this normal? This looks very *un-normal* to me."

Eleutherios stared at me a second before reluctantly answering, "I've never seen a storm like this. This circle of clearness, it is…unnatural. I fear we are ensorcelled." Her eyes stared out the bridge toward the dark and roiling wall bearing down on us on the other side of the eye. Within it, flash after flash of lightning spasmodically erupted, like the skies over the Catatumbo River during one of its legendary displays.

That gnawing feeling in my gut returned. "You said that the empress had ordered your mission, correct?"

"Yes," she responded quizzically.

"Was it the empress, or one of her servants?"

"Of course it wasn't her directly; it was Phalinos, her sorcerer."

"Phalinos," I repeated resignedly, and her eyes lit up with revelation.

"What does he have against you?" she blurted out. I looked at the rapidly approaching wall of darkness. I didn't answer. "Whatever it is, it looks like it's enough to try to kill you over it," the captain surmised. She turned her gaze back to the water. "I'm going to stay in this clearing as long as I can and hope that the storm peters out before we're forced into the catastrophe that lies ahead."

I rushed down to the cabin and informed Zew and Diana of the captain's course and my suspicions about Phalinos. "He'd try it," Zew stated bluntly. "He's always distrusted my existence, and I wouldn't be surprised if he felt pushed over the edge by my recent reappearance."

"But how can he do this?" I questioned. "This is way beyond what I thought possible for a sorcerer—I thought they dealt with ghosts and such."

"He's the Imperial Sorcerer, Stonewall. That means he has access to over two centuries of New Greece's accumulated magics. Our forebears made pacts with the natural spirits of the islands and sea—that's part of why they're so bountiful. Perhaps he's made another bargain, called in some favors, made some promises?" Zew posited.

"Do you think the captain can keep us in this 'eye' you speak of?" Diana asked.

"If this was a normal storm, we'd have a good chance, but I don't want to speculate if this is a magically-created storm," I answered honestly. "Regardless, I agree with the captain and would rather try to stay in the eye than plow through the wall."

They decided to see for themselves and clambered on deck. A sheet of grim, towering clouds peppered with scintillating lightning encircled us, and my companions were stunned at the display. Their faces dropped once they understood the dangers ahead. "That's not right," Zew gasped, jabbing a finger at the wall of the eye. "I've never seen a storm like that, and I've spent more than a century on this sea, sailing every nook and cranny of her coasts."

We stood and stared at the display for a long while, the breeze rippling our clothes. Our heading had changed to the north, but by doing so, the captain was able to keep the point-class cutter out of the looming clouds for hours until the sun started going down. In the fading light, we realized maintaining our position was going to be difficult—in the dark cloudy night, only a ring of lightning guided our captain's choices.

It seemed wise to prepare for the worst, and we loaded up

my medikit with anything that needed to stay out of the water, like the invisibility powder. Despite the fact that it had a zipper, the medikit was waterproof; it's remarkable what late twenty-third-century tech can accomplish. I was surprised when Diana fished out a small leather book for inclusion; I'd never seen her reading it and she didn't look like the type that kept a diary. I packed it into the medikit without further probing—if she'd wanted me to know, she'd have told me.

With that sorted, we puzzled about what to do with the pounds of gold we each had littered about our bodies in what was called coin strips. Sentients beneath the shattered moon had a particular way of placing coins on thin strips of cloth and then twisting them so they didn't come out or clang against each other. The strips were then wrapped about the body to distribute weight, which was going to be a problem if we ended up needing to swim. Diana came up with a simple solution that had failed to occur to either Zew or I: tying off our coin strips in a slip knot around our upper torso so that a single tug on the release strip at our sternum would release the bunch.

The dying of the light required the use of my flashlight to finish settling all our gear, and by the time we were ready for the worst, the ship started jumping again. Try as she might, Eleutherios couldn't keep us perfectly in the center of the eye. Each time we strayed toward the edge, the cutter would lurch and lunge with the push and pull of the storm's wall before a burst of power from the engine beneath us put us back in calmer waters. This process repeated itself for several hours as we huddled in our cabin, occasionally hearing the yells of the crew and captain through the watertight door.

A little after midnight—shortly after we'd decided it was relatively safe to try for sleep—the yells from outside the cabin intensified and *Agōgós* turned sharply, rolling us in our bunks despite being tied in. "What the...?" was all I got out before I felt the bottom of the ship drop out and I was suddenly weightless for a fraction of a second, like when your plane hits turbulence. It ended with a solid thunk—the sound of rock on metal. I was certain we were going down, but I was wrong. A second later, the cutter tilted twenty-five degrees forward and then rolled back and forth before finally settling motionless for the first time since we boarded.

I unhooked myself from the bunk and scrambled to the deck, amazed by what greeted me: the sky dark was cloudless, a black canvas splashed with thousands of stars, and the air was still and cool. The *Agōgós* was a good forty yards away and ten feet above the water's edge, as if it had been plucked by the hands of an angry god and planted upon the shore like a toy. The high-water mark on the beach was distressingly close to the water, showing that even at high tide, the ship would remain dry-docked. Behind me, the gasps of Zew and Diana matched those coming out of the bridge as Eleutherios and her first mate, Periclymenus, swung open their door and gazed out into the serene nocturnal backdrop that greeted us.

"We're on the Isle," Periclymenus blurted. "The storm's pushed us onto the Isle, and now we're all dead men!" His wild-eyed face raged as he thrust his fingers at us. "It's your fault! We're dead and it's all your fault!"

Chapter Seventeen

The Isle of Doom

The sun dawned while we were taking everything out of the ship that could prove useful. Eleutherios did her best to calm her crew, and once everyone understood we were in this together, the initial animosity hurled at us lessened but didn't completely disappear. If things got too bad, I planned to let them know who Zew really was and then watch them change their tune, but that was a last resort to keep them from attacking us. I'd gotten the distinct impression from both Zew and the empress that the fewer sentients that knew a member of House Zelos was still alive, the better for everyone, but if it was my butt on the line, they could deal with the repercussions of publicity.

We didn't need to pull everything out of the ship—it wasn't going anywhere—but I've always found it best to physically take inventory and lay hands on everything available to you in a survival situation. Often times when the need arises, an item could be repurposed into an alternate use than it was intended or designed for, but that only works if you remember everything you've got and physically understood the nature of your resources and requirements.

Unfortunately, taking stock revealed some stark news: we only had enough food for three days. Thankfully, we had ample fishing line and hooks, and the Isle of Doom was large so we should be able to hunt and gather for the rest. Unlike other island castaways, we also had the benefit of sailing freshwater seas and would be spared the wretched fate of mariners on the open seas: water, water everywhere, nor any drop to drink.

We'd landed on a long sandy beach that claimed a section of a large bay, but much of the island itself was hilly with patches of wood. With any luck, there were some larger ungulates further inland, and possibly a deep cave that would make better lodging than the *Agōgós* should we have to overwinter on the isle. The cutter would do fine for a while, but the bitter cold and winds of deep winter would turn it into a metallic freezer in time.

Once I brought these salient points to everyone's attention, the captain and crew regarded me differently. Diana and Zew were used to my constant threat assessments and contingency plans, but our Greek companions had little idea just how fortunate they were —if you had to be stranded on the Isle of Doom, you wanted to be stranded with someone like me.

Having one of the three rifles, I volunteered to go hunting and start scouting out the nearby area while everyone else put our materials back into place. I trudged a mile to the largest of the gentle hills and pulled out my binoculars once I reached the top. I got my first good look at our surroundings: sparsely wooded sloping hills in all directions. To the northeast, about ten miles away, a thick forest sprouted up, covering rougher land that eventually turned into what could be called mountains, but more of the Appalachian-type than the Andean. There was a noticeable lack of rivers or streams, which meant that any game on the island had to come to shore to drink.

I breathed a sigh of relief when I spotted several small herds of deer during my scan. That took a lot of weight off my shoulders. The chances of a ship coming by during this time of the year were next to nil, and without food, things would have quickly gotten grim. I hated to waste ammunition to down a deer, but it would help morale—the sooner we got food the better—so I got a beautiful eight-point in my sights and pulled the trigger on my M24 sniper rifle.

Nothing happened.

I checked the rifle and the ammunition, but everything seemed in working order. I loaded up another round and tried once more. Again, nothing happened. *Oh, this isn't good, this isn't good at all.* Hoping I was wrong, I drew my M1B plasma blaster and pulled the trigger. Nothing happened. I tested my plasma cutter and found that it didn't work, either.

And now I knew why it was called the Isle of Doom. Without modern weapons or tools, things would be significantly rougher. I did more testing and found out it was only weapons or things that could easily be used as weapons that didn't work. My other pieces of tech, like my binoculars and ghillie suit, still worked fine. I didn't know why it was that way, and having no other logical reasons, I jumped to the go-to solution for strangeness beneath the shattered moon: magic. My mind leapt to all the ancient Greek myths and stories, and I thought it best to join the others before I found a labyrinth sporting a minotaur or got turned into a pig by Circe's great-great-granddaughter.

I was halfway back to the *Agōgós* when I heard yelling from the direction of the ship. I picked up the pace—I couldn't make out what was being said but it sounded serious. As I crossed the final hill a few minutes later, I caught sight of four bodies lying next to our tilting and beached ship, pools of blood staining the white sand beneath them. I sprinted the remaining distance and dropped down next to the bodies, double-checking that there wasn't anything I could do.

"We were attacked by a herd of cloudhorses," Diana explained as I checked the first of fallen. "Our firearms didn't work, so we had to clear them out by hand. Castor, Idas, Butes, and Hylas went down before we sent the cloudhorses packing, the ones we didn't kill, that is." The Blade Witch nudged her head along the beach where six dead cloudhorses lay.

Cloudhorses were a fusion of nanotechnology with the biological base of a seahorse and a common lizard, bearing only a passing resemblance to either. Rather, they were slender and almost snake-like, with a sharp spike at the end of their tail and sharp teeth in their seahorse-like head. They were amphibious, birthing in the water, but spent most of their lives in the air.

By all rationality, their short stubby wings should never be able to hold their forty-pound bodies aloft, but then again, I've also seen a pigman fly under the shattered moon, so what do I know?

I hadn't encountered cloudhorses, but according to the books in the Library, they were unpleasant and aggressive creatures—dumb as a post and just as durable. They hunted in groups using a sort of hypnotism to freeze their prey in place before stabbing with their tails. They also attacked whenever hungry or threatened, although their threat assessment was loosely tethered to reality. One book illustrated the point by reporting cases of cloudhorses attacking trees, because apparently a tree can appear aggressive in the eyes of a cloudhorse.

"How many fled? How many did you drive away?" I quizzed Diana as I closed the fallen Greek's eyes.

"Only four were left. I don't think they'll return, but I could be wrong," Diana replied as she wiped down her twin blades.

I nodded and went on to the next body. Diana covered me as I checked for signs of life, but there were none. While I was finishing with the last corpse, an argument broke out between the captain and Periclymenus, muffled shouting from behind the closed door of the bridge. I couldn't make out what was said until Periclymenus threw the door open. "I'm done with this. I'm going home. Best of luck!"

"If you go, you'll be named as a deserter!" Eleutherios shouted.

"By whom?" he taunted. "They'll believe anything I tell them because you'll be dead—sorry, Captain, but I'm not going down with the ship." He turned and ran down the length of the ship before jumping off the stern, turning into a hawk before he hit the sand, and flying out to sea.

"At least tell them we're here, you bastard!" Eleutherios yelled with a raised fist.

There was a time when a guy changing into a hawk would have dumbfounded me. Not anymore. I guess I may have finally turned native, because no one else around me seemed overtly fazed by the event, either, and now I fit right in. We just looked up at the captain, waiting to see what she'd do. There were only three other crewmen left: Phocus, the shy intelligent type who anticipated orders and who took care of the engine; Hypatia, the muscle of the bunch who occasionally had to be told to do something twice; and Telesilla, who I hadn't quite pinned down yet, but my gut had her pegged as the most dangerous of the bunch.

"Let's get them buried a hundred yards south of here near the top of the beach to keep scavengers away," the captain ordered, grabbing one of the dinghy's oars as a makeshift shovel. We didn't need to do anything about the cloudhorse corpses—they'd dissolve into goo after a few hours and be completely gone in less than a day.

We grabbed the dead and dragged them south. I stripped the clothing off them before burying them; it may seem mercenary, but we might need the extra layers when the weather turned. I washed the clothes in the water to get out the blood and draped them across the side of the *Agōgós* to dry in the sun. By the time everything was done, it was noon, and we shared a tense lunch huddled near the fire we'd built next to the ship.

"We don't have any melee weapons other than our knives, and perhaps the two gaffs," Eleutherios responded to Zew's question. He'd traded in his pilgrim's staff for a proper spear before leaving Naxos, Diana always had her swords, and I always had my KM6800 fighting utility knife.

"If you want, I could bend the ends of the gaffs off and sharpen the remaining metal into spears. They won't be the best, but they'll work and two more of us will be armed," I offered.

"I'll help," Hypatia volunteered, and we set to work while the others discussed various ideas for survival between the sounds of us scraping the metal gaffs against stone. The general consensus was that we should try fishing as much as we could, using insects and worms as bait. Everyone's eyes lit up when I unscrewed the hilt of my KM6800 and showed them the three shiny hooks along with the accompanying fishing wire. The ship had its own fishing supplies, but they were larger than what I had and this close to shore, smaller hooks should get better results.

It took through lunch to get the spears into shape and once I finished with mine, I handed it to the captain. She distributed it to Telesilla, confirming my suspicion that she was the dangerous type, and Hypatia kept hers. That done, we collected some bait and pulled the dinghy down from the side of the *Agōgós*, pushing it into the water for some close-to-shore fishing. The dinghy could fit eight, but since we only had three hooks, I was joined by Diana and Hypatia.

We'd fished for a half hour or so, catching three good-sized yellow perch, when inspiration hit me. "Mind your ears," I warned my companions as I unslung my rifle. "I have an idea…" And sure enough, it fired when I pulled the trigger. I whooped victoriously, not the least bit bothered that I was scaring away the fish. "This means we can hunt for deer from the boat. You know they have to come to the shore to drink!"

Chapter Eighteen

Footprints in the Sand

Let it never be said that I am not thorough. I discovered that I couldn't fire while standing in the water, nor could I fire when I was in the boat if it was touching shore, but as long as the boat was completely in the water, the rifle worked. The realization that deer were on the menu lifted the mood, and when both Zew and Diana vouched that I was the best shot they'd ever seen, the crewmembers burst out with some real smiles, the first since the *Agōgós* beached.

We got back to fishing once I was satisfied with my grasp of the "rules" of the Isle of Doom, and we came back to land with a half-dozen perch and one ten-pound walleye. While we'd fished, the others completed their local scout, traveling in a group to dissuade any remaining cloudhorses. They didn't find anyplace worthy of a winter shelter, but they only covered one of three directions, so we still had a chance to get lucky.

Dinner was fresh fish cooked on sticks and we'd caught a little more than we needed, so we ate till we were overfull; the safest place to store excess food is in the stomach. After eating, we collected more firewood, stacking it within the ship to keep it dry before we retired to the crew bunks—with safety in numbers, we decided to all sleep together behind the watertight doors as long as the weather was still bearable. I fell asleep trying to figure out how long it would take us to dig out the *Agōgós* if we set our mind to it based upon the amount of time it took to dig the graves for Castor, Idas, Butes, and Hylas. Now that I figured out how to use my plasma cutter just off the coast of this blasted island, I could quickly make a wide variety of digging tools, and if half of us acquired food while the other half worked...

The next morning was cold and our breath steamed as we waited by the fire for our part of the pot of beans. A beneficial side effect of yesterday's tragedy was that culling our numbers nearly in half had almost doubled our days of food rations, but we were still perilously low. During breakfast, I put forth my idea of digging a canal for the *Agōgós* before full winter hit.

"Based on how the amount of time it took us to bury the crew, we should be able to do it in two months...but more realistically, with proper digging tools I can manufacture with the plasma cutter, it should be around a month."

"That's cutting it close," Eleutherios cautioned. "Come December, the northern parts of the Center Sea freeze over and if it takes us even two weeks longer than that, there's a chance we won't be able to get out no matter what we do. Plus, if we're still digging when the freezes hit, the ground's going to be harder and digging will be slower." I deferred to her greater familiarly with the local weather, but posited another approach.

They all looked at me strangely while I went to the dingy and pushed myself into the water. I heard Zew mutter under his breath as I went out, "Bear with him, he's got a plan. He's a castaway—mad as a hatter but crafty in his own way."

I grinned at his vote of confidence as I roped the plasma cutter to one of the impromptu fishing rods and turned it on. I leaned over the edge of boat, pushing the rod out over the land. I was able to draw the plasma blade through the ground. "Eureka!" I shouted—I couldn't stop myself from making the historic exclamation in its proper language—yet surprisingly, none of the Greeks got it; must be different timeline Greeks.

"As long as *I'm* not touching the earth, I can use the cutter at a distance. All I'll need to do is build up a cantilever and balance it. I should be able to extend my reach twenty, maybe thirty feet. But the easier solution would be to make a canal that allows the dingy to float right up to where it needs to be. With this thing, I can cut through rocks, frozen earth, anything. It should make digging much faster—maybe only two, three weeks."

Eleutherios grinned. "All right, you've convinced me. Let's get moving on this; once you've made the tools, we'll get digging. After that, you should take the dingy out with Phocus and fish around the island. Keep moving around and watch the shores for any game you can take with your rifle. We need more food."

Between Zew, Diana, Hypatia, and myself, we dragged

most of a fallen tree into the water, allowing me to cut it into sections. I made quick work, carving out various tools from blocks of wood: digging sticks with a footstep; a wooden version of the adze that should be good to "cut" off slices of earth; and deep basin shovels to help haul the sand and dirt away. Every time I sliced the wood, it would flame from the heat of the cutter, but I had plenty of water for quenching. I made enough tools for everyone as well as an extra set in case of breakage before cutting a second tree into firewood, throwing each piece onto shore as I finished with it. It was much easier than gathering wood and once it was stacked in the *Agōgós*, it would dry out.

Next, Phocus and I hunted down some bait and rowed around the western end of the bay. The circumstances of our arrival didn't lend itself to clear sight of land, so I took the opportunity to scout a bit before settling in to fish after a few miles of rowing. Around the bay was a long grassy slope leading to the water's edge and if deer were going to water nearby, this would be an ideal spot—they wouldn't like the open beach we'd landed on and preferred to remain in tall grasses for concealment.

During the next few hours, we caught another eighteen fish—there must not be a lot of easy food out here as the fish were very amenable to our hooked bait—and Phocus outfished me three to one. No deer approached the shore while we fished but the tracks on the shore were proof that they watered here, if only occasionally. If it was only a matter of timing, I could come back at dusk or dawn when they were more active.

It was a bit past noon when we returned to our camp and the proof of concept was unmistakable: the digging crew had already carved a five-foot-long canal leading toward the *Agōgós*. Everyone knew the first part would be the easiest going, but there was a palpable sense of accomplishment as we devoured the freshly roasted fish. I convinced the group to let Phocus stay on fishing duty since he'd performed so well, and we gathered more bait before hitting the water again with promises to return after dusk.

There were fewer fish this time around, but I managed to bag a ten-point buck. Not wanting to expose myself to scavengers with only a knife for protection while I dressed the deer, I dragged it into the water and tied it to the dingy for the twenty-minute row back to camp. I was pleasantly surprised to find the canal had progressed another five feet and steered the dingy through it, beaching the small boat at the canal's end. If the group had been happy to see us return with the fish for lunch, the deer made them ecstatic. We cut off portions and skewered them over the fire as we had with the fish; it was an elegant, if primitive, cooking method.

"It looks like this could really work," Eleutherios remarked as I butchered the deer. "We've made more progress than I thought we could."

"There's little that determined sentients who refuse to

surrender cannot accomplish," Zew declared. "We will see Alexandria before winter."

"Since we got a deer, Phocus and I will be on digging duty tomorrow and that will move us along even faster," I added encouragingly. Everyone knows that water, shelter, and warmth are the keys to wilderness survival, but the gauge used to measure success is morale. You're more likely to succeed if you can maintain a positive mood, even if you're lacking one or more of the survival requirements. Diana and Zew were indomitable, so I didn't worry about them, but I wasn't certain about the crew. I had to think they were hardened to deprivation, as members of the Imperial Navy, but judging on how quickly Periclymenus flew the coop, I couldn't be sure.

"Tomorrow, I bet we could double what was done today. Let's get out of here as soon as possible," I postulated between bites of crispy venison. Daily goals often motivate better than longer ones, and soon the chatter turned to options about how to clear and level the *Agōgós* before the canal arrived. We compared ideas for a few hours before heading off to bed, storing the cleaned deer carcass in the captain's quarters to prevent attracting scavengers. We fell asleep quickly—a hard day's labor makes for heavy sleep—and I rose before the others the next morning. I quietly slipped out of the crew's quarters without waking the others. It was another cold one and I was about to hop over the edge of the ship and stoke up the fire when I discovered the tracks.

The footprints were human-shaped, except they were three-feet long and with four toes. They'd come from inland sometime during the night, walked around the *Agōgós* and then to the south. Whatever made them had a stride of eight feet, which made it roughly eighteen feet tall if it conformed to human anatomy. If it did, we had a giant; if it didn't, I had no idea what it could be, even with all my studies in the Library.

I leapt off the ship and followed the tracks to the south, nervous about what I'd find. Sure enough, the grave was disturbed and all the corpses missing. We had a man-eater, which made me think it might be a cyclops. Even though the literature described them as only twice the height of a man, it continually harped upon their desire for human flesh, preferably consumed after several days of putrefaction.

I followed the tracks until they entered the grassland to the west and then returned to the ship to trace the origins of the tracks. The incoming footprints originated from the northeast, which was more wooded and rougher terrain than the other directions. It was par for the course; I couldn't see a cyclops lairing in the grassy soft hills when a cave might be available.

Although the cyclops's footprints were my primary worry, they weren't the only tracks on the beach. I'd seen two deer tracks, two very large dog tracks, a bear track, and rather a lot of rabbit tracks, which made me worry about the ubiquitous bunnyshark. The canine tracks were large and tended to move with the cyclops's steps, so I marked them down as pets of some sort. I hoped they were mundane mutts, but the size of the paw that made those imprints in the sand made me think about demon dogs—massive, foul-tempered, intelligent, dog-like fairies. I preferred to think we were only dealing with one intelligent enemy rather than several. Demon dogs usually dwelled in ruins or in swamps and so far I'd seen neither, so I put them as less likely than just your average, every day, souped-up English mastiff.

I got the fire going, put a few pounds of beans in the pot, and waited for the rest of the group to wake.

Chapter Nineteen

The Hunter and the Hunted

The crew was remarkably calm when I revealed our nocturnal visitor. I expected a little more reaction to the news of a man-eating cyclops visiting our camp in the night on the Isle of Doom, but in retrospect, is there anything more Greek than that? Or perhaps they were too exhausted to get riled up about anything that wasn't a clear and present danger.

"I thought I smelled something different today," Phocus remarked casually. "There have always been legends about cyclopes on the isle."

"Smelled?" I puzzled.

"I've got a really good sense of smell—part of the reason why I prefer being on the water than on land," he explained while stirring the pot of beans over the fire.

I raised an eyebrow. "Do you think you could track the cyclops by smell?"

The engineer shifted uncomfortably. "Maybe, if I had to, now that I've got its scent," he admitted reluctantly. Remember how I said the crew was calm about the cyclops situation? Apparently, cyclopes are fine in the abstract sense, but when you go asking questions about tracking them down, things are not so copacetic. I backed off once I detected cracks in their serenity and focused on our breakfast of venison and beans—poor Phocus's nose!

With warm food in our bellies, we hit the ground running. The canal had gotten deep enough that we started unearthing larger stones, which significantly slowed down progress. As I was the strongest, I spent the morning pulling out the big stones that others found as well as deepening the existing parts of the canal—it was easier for me to move the heavy wet soil under the water line while the others chipped away at the easier stuff above the water, advancing the canal closer to the *Agōgós*.

We ran into complications twice during the morning, but it was nothing my dangling plasma cutter couldn't cut through. Balanced out over the dinghy, the work was unwieldy and took five times longer than normal, but it worked and the digging progressed. The water started off cold as hell, but with all the exertion, it became bearable. I still crowded around the fire when it was lunchtime; once I was out of the water, evaporation and a little wind made it seem colder than it was.

After lunch, I climbed to the top of the *Agōgós* and took a quick look around with my binoculars. Nothing exciting was happening, but I discovered what looked to be a trail through the rough terrain under the woods to the northeast that I hadn't seen from the small hill I'd trekked to earlier. Perhaps this was where the cyclops came from? Earlier, I'd only traced the cyclops's footprints to the end of the beach to make sure it wasn't an immediate threat.

I quietly called Diana and Zew up to take a look and they agreed that it was definitely a trail, and a big one at that, judging from its width compared to that of the nearby trees. We decided to notify the rest of the group, each taking turns with my binoculars. While it didn't change the potential threat of the man-eater, knowing just that bit of information seemed to soothe their nerves. Information parity was a powerful boon in these types of situations. Sure, it knew where we were, but now we knew where it was, too, or rather where it traveled to get to us and how to track it down if need be.

The captain quickly put an end to our lollygagging with a curt, "Come on, this ship isn't going to dig itself out!" By dinner, we'd lengthened, widened, and deepened the canal. We were now almost halfway to our goal and the part closest to shore was wide enough for the *Agōgós* to pass though although not deep enough. With concrete progress before us, morale was high around the fire. The digging would slow down significantly from this point, but it looked like our plan would work and there was a levity among us that had been absent since our arrival on the Isle. Telesilla even sang a song for us, and although her voice wasn't anything to write home about, we all appreciated the bit of cheer she brought into the gloaming.

The discussion became serious before we turned into bed. We'd decided that I should spend the night on the dinghy about fifty yards out in the bay, anchored by a rope secured around a heavy rock. With a functioning rifle, I should be able to fend off an attack if it came to that. It meant a night of little sleep after and before days of hard work, but it was the only way to be safe, and if need be, I'd have to become nocturnal while we struggled to get off the isle. I took my night vision binoculars and ghillie suit with me; both in combination would allow me to keep watch without being seen and the distance should cover my scent—if the cyclops or his dogs picked up the scent, they would likely think it was coming from those camped in the cutter.

While the others tucked into their sleeping quarters for a comfortable night's rest, I floated off shore, once again using the suit as a blanket while scanning the beach in night vision. It was a calm night, waves lapped at the dinghy like playful Chihuahuas nipping at the sides of the boat. I set up a series of alarms in my internal clock to ensure I stayed awake—it beat being shaken by pilgrims, but only by a hair.

Around midnight, Eleutherios came out of the cabin for her nightly piss. She wasn't as young as the rest of us—Zew excluded, but he seemed locked in at a physical age of about thirty-five—and she never made it through the night without going at least once. We'd worried about the cyclops or its dogs taking her out while she was doing her business as our shared latrine was further out and somewhat secluded for privacy. Accordingly, I set up a small privy for her that was closer to the ship and shore. It was out in the open so she couldn't be ambushed and I could cover her from the dinghy. One uneventful piss later, I breathed a sigh of relief as the captain made her way back to the ship without incident.

I've spent a lot of time surveilling and executing stealth maneuvers as Agent Six, and one of the truisms I've encountered is that 2:00–4:00 a.m. are the best hours to do anything covert. By then, people are almost universally asleep—even the majority of those having a late night—and it's still too early for even the earliest of risers. They are the witching hours for us spies, and the fact that the cyclops and his two massive dogs came upon the *Agōgós* shortly after 2:30 made me think that he could be smarter—or more cunning—than his rudimentary appearance suggested.

The cyclops was close to eighteen feet tall and at least nine feet wide at the shoulder. He had a wide face and a protruding jaw, more Neanderthal than human but definitely in the same family, save the single ocular orifice. The giant eye dominated the center of his bulging face, and his arms reached down to his knees. He was clad in wooly white sheepskins roughly sewn with strips of leather—and this made me think that where there are sheep, there are shepherds...if the cyclops was not one himself. He welded a primitive tree-like spear with a fire-hardened tip that was slightly taller than himself, although the brute strength in his limbs would be more than enough weaponry in melee.

He reached down and absentmindedly petted his two canines with a scratch behind their ears in a simple gesture of companionship. The dogs were five feet at the shoulder and built like bulldogs—I shuddered to think how big they would get if these were puppies. The trio came down to the *Agōgós* and sniffed around. I couldn't tell how noisy they were over the sound of the waves, but the cyclops was deliberate in his steps, going slow and checking the ground before putting his foot down; I bet this was what I looked like to passing rodents when I'm sneaking around. After circumambulating the ship, he inspected the canal while one of his long limbs stroked his chin. He stood there silently for a few minutes and then moved south to inspect the graves he'd previously emptied. Finding no new inhabitants, he moved deeper into the isle and eventually disappeared into the hills.

The remainder of the night passed uneventfully and when morning broke, I rowed to shore and rekindled the fire for breakfast while I waited for everyone to rouse. They took most of the information in stride, but everyone agreed that the giant's inspection of the canal was worrisome; if he decided to sabotage our work, we'd be forced into a conflict.

"It won't come to that," I promised. "If he does anything aggressive or hostile, I'll put him down."

"Perhaps you should just kill him first," Hypatia suggested.

Zew and Diana nodded their agreement, as did Telesilla.

"Take him out before he attacks," Diana summed up her stance.

"I could, but if he's not really bothering us I'd rather not jump straight to preemptive killing." I looked toward Phocus and Eleutherios to see what they thought about Hypatia's suggestion. Phocus was unreadable—he kept his cards close to his chest on the best of days—but Eleutherios's body language seemed to favor the suggestion. "If all he does is come looking for buried dead, there is no need to kill him, and if he doesn't come back to shore, killing him would involve hunting him down in the forest or his lair with only our spears. I don't know about you, but I don't really feel the need to explore more of the Isle of Doom than necessary."

A silent moment of thought hovered over the fire before Eleutherios weighed in. "There is merit in your position and I agree looking for trouble is hardly worth it, especially with the progress we have made with the canal and getting back out to sea before winter. I can tell you'd rather not, but if you are as good a shot as they say you are"—the captain nodded toward at Zew and Diana—"you'd be better for the job than anyone else here; it would be done quick and clean. If it must be done, it should be you."

I'd admired the captain's nautical acumen ever since she kept the cutter from shattering to pieces in the hurricane, but now I saw her diplomatic savvy. She wasn't ordering me to do it, yet somehow, *I* would seem like the jerk if I refused. Outnumbered, I relented. "How about I keep the rifle ready for tomorrow night and if he does anything untoward, I'll kill him then. But he's got to *do* something; just being nosy isn't enough for me to pull the trigger."

My answer seemed acceptable to everyone but Hypatia. "Because raiding the graves of our friends and eating their corpses isn't *doing* enough!" she fumed. I could tell that if she had a rifle, she'd do it herself, but the others gave me the benefit of the doubt so she angrily went along with them. As a general rule, everyone was fine with a convenient murder when someone else was pulling the trigger. They didn't want blood on their hands, so they let me set my conditions.

I was glad to return to digging; the breakfast conversation reminded me too much of my time as Agent Six—discussing the terms and conditions of a hit. Now that I knew for certain that going back to my time was impossible, I saw little reason to keep Agent Six alive. William Stonewall may have all that guy's abilities and advantages, but he didn't kill indiscriminately.

I lost myself in physical exertion, pushing myself to a place where the higher brain functions didn't work and nothing was more important that moving another shovelful of sand and dirt. In that space, I couldn't think about anything but the movements my task required. Lunch came quickly and even with all our effort, we'd only gained a few more feet; as we moved up the beach, the volume of material that needed excavating seemed to increase exponentially. I was silent at lunch, letting the others talk as I scarfed down the meal so I could return to motion as quickly as possible.

By the time night fell, we'd gained only five feet and they decided to change our digging tactics tomorrow; instead of digging the canal in one run, a group would "pre-dig" from the *Agōgós* to the end of the canal. In this way, they hoped to reduce the hardest digging by lowering the volume of earth moved out of the deepest part of the canal. It was a good idea, and I simply grunted my approval before climbing back into the dinghy for another restless night. I didn't feel much like participating.

Given last night's activities, I took a calculated risk and grabbed three hours of sleep right when I anchored in the bay, waking up to my internal alarm—for which I am forever thankful—just before midnight. The night had turned cloudy and the wind had picked up, pushing the dingy up and over foot-tall waves, not enough to worry about but just enough to make it to uncomfortable. Oh well, I'd been uncomfortable before.

The night passed silently; Eleutherios woke for her nightly toilet, a herd of deer appeared on the far side of the bay for a drink followed by a trio of bunnysharks, patiently waiting for any show of weakness from the deer, and a massive bird flew by just below the clouds. The bird was raptorial and truly huge, with something like a sixty-foot wingspan. I couldn't be certain, but I assumed it was one of the giant eagles from the Eagle Lord's territory. Located on the northeastern coast of the Center Sea, the Eagle Lord's territory was surrounded by Great

Suomi. Geographically, it would make sense for them to hunt out here, but this was the first giant bird I had seen in the sky over the western part of the Isle of Doom, where we'd wrecked.

I was especially vigilant as 2:00 a.m. neared and sure enough, the cyclops returned. This time, he carried a massive spade instead of a spear and I silently cursed his decision as I readied my rifle. I waited for him to seal his fate with a single shovelful of dirt before shooting through his eye and the thin bones behind his massive orb, downing him with a single shot.

His fall set off his dogs. They started running around, barking and growling, looking for an enemy. They were well trained enough to understand what had happened, so I rose from the boat and yelled for them to go away, hoping they would get the message. Instead, they charged me, fearlessly diving into the waves and paddling toward the dinghy. Another two shots took care of the problem. I was halfway to the shore by the time everyone got out of their bunks and onto the deck.

Chapter Twenty

Half Out of the Cave

I dragged the dingy onto the sand and joined the crowd surrounding the dead cyclops. "Could you have killed something bigger, Stonewall?" Diana joked as I arrived. I looked down at the sprawled giant and the massive shovel he would have used to quickly undo our work.

"I'm going to sleep," I replied. And I did.

When I awoke, the crew had already dragged the cyclops to the old gravesite and buried him under a foot or two of sand and dirt. It wouldn't prevent determined scavengers, but it would keep the opportunists away, and more importantly, the smell. I ate a piece of cold venison in silence and quickly joined the digging already in progress.

During lunch, Phocus broached the subject of raiding the cyclops's cave for valuables. "If you've already killed him and the dogs, there shouldn't be anything there, and it can't be more than ten miles away. I could track us there if we left after lunch and then we could come back by nightfall, or spend the night there if everything's safe." His tone and rapid speech indicated nervousness, that he had wanted to say something earlier but had to work up his courage first.

"It would have been better to go earlier," Diana pointed out. "We'd have more light and wouldn't have to worry about getting back. We could just wait till tomorrow morning."

"That's what I thought of doing, but now I don't know if we'll have the chance." He looked up at the darkening sky. "If it rains too much, I'll lose the scent. My nose is not nearly as good as a dog's."

Everyone looked at me—apparently being the cyclops's killer gave me the final word on the looting. I shrugged. "It sounds like a good idea to me. The sheepskins on the cyclops looked to be domesticated, so there's a good chance we can get some mutton out of it, if nothing else."

With the possibility of mutton on dinner's menu, we rushed through the rest of lunch and hit the trail: Phocus in the lead, followed by Diana and Zew, then Telesilla, Eleutherios, myself, and finally Hypatia. Phocus led us up the beach and over the low surrounding hill before turning toward the rougher, wooded part of the isle where we suspected the cyclops had resided.

The walk proved a long one, but Phocus's nose was true—he quickly found the path we'd previously seen through the binoculars, and never hesitated nor took more than a second to determine which of the several forks to follow. We kept our eyes out for wild animals or worse, but encountered none; I wouldn't be surprised if the presence of the cyclops had something to do with that.

After two hours of hiking, we encountered an eight-foot-tall stone wall reminiscent of old New England construction: placed stone construction without mortar or joinery. I quickly climbed on top and found a well-tended pasture on the other side of the wall. Several hundred sheep were corralled in the hundred or so acres enclosed by the massive wall. Even by cyclopean standards, this was a major project that would have taken years to complete.

We happened to be near the area where the sheep could go up one ramp and then down another to exit the pen. There was a wooden drawbridge halfway up the interior ramp which prevented the sheep from exiting if it wasn't lowered. It was crudely built but elegant in function, much like the stone wall.

I informed the group of my find and descended. We headed toward the exterior part of the sheep ramp, still following Phocus's nose, and then east into a rugged, almost karst-like landscape. We traversed a hundred yards before we found the cave entrance: a twelve-foot-tall opening concealed by a quartet of trees whose roots dangled over the side of the cliff. Their ends had been meticulously trimmed, preventing them from touching the ground and eventually closing off the cave. The pendulous roots sprouted leaves, although this late in the year, only a few dry and desperate hangers on remained. I imagined the greenery would have completely covered the entrance during the height of summer. It was remarkably difficult to spot considering how big it was, and were it not for

Phocus's sensitive nose and the many sheep tracks, we could have unknowingly walked right by it in other circumstances.

Once we discovered the cave, Zew, Diana, and Hypatia moved to the front and entered three abroad, spears forward. We followed behind them once they signaled the all clear. After narrowing at the entrance, the underground passage opened into a large, pungent chamber; although the cyclops may have been housetrained, his dogs certainly weren't. The chamber had a sleeping area composed of dozens of poorly-tanned sheepskins, a cold fire pit under a spit roast large enough for said sheep, and a curved passage leading deeper into the rock. The corridor was lit on the far side, so wherever it went, it was open to the sky. Our trio of fighters cautiously descended toward the light. They'd gone no more than thirty feet before the silence was rent by a piercing scream that knocked back all of us. It sounded like the cry of a raptor, and at that volume, it could only be one of the giant eagles.

"'Ware the beak!" Zew cried out from around the bend as I rushed to the front. The passage expanded into an even larger space open to the air, and this chamber was several times bigger than the previous one. In the center was a giant eagle lying on its side, captive under a crude net of woven tree roots. It was unable to use either feet or wings; however, it retained full movement of its neck and head. Our three warriors artfully dodged its lurches and kept their weapons readied but did not attack the trapped avian.

Even to my untrained eye, the eagle looked to be in bad shape. It was thin with dull feathers sticking out in all directions. Given the amount of its own waste encircling it, it must have been here for a long time. The cave continued downward via another passage, but getting to it required entering the range of the giant eagle's fearsome beak.

"Free me!" it suddenly spoke, in perfect Finnish. Its voice was harsh and composed of three tones: the first, third, and fifth of a precise major chord.

Surprisingly, I was the least-shocked of the group and responded first, "We will, but first we're going to feed you as many sheep as you think you can eat. How many should we kill?"

Zew and Diana immediately understood my order of operations and the others were quick to catch on—if you're going free a massive predator, you should stuff it with food before you free it, especially if it's been starved in captivity.

"Six," the bird replied in its melodic voice.

"All right, let's go wrangle up some sheep everyone," I ordered the rest of the group. Once we were out of the cave, we started talking freely, assuming the giant eagle couldn't hear us. Everyone was in favor of freeing the creature on principle, but worries abounded. In the end, we reached the conclusion that when the time came to cut the eagle free, we should minimize exposure to danger. Being the strongest and most agile, I volunteered to cut the bindings while everyone else waited outside. Most of the Greeks seemed fine with this arrangement, but Zew and Diana would have none of it—they told me to shove it and that they'd be there even if I didn't want them. Hypatia also refused to be shunted out of the action, and I would be lying if I said I didn't feel better having some backup.

It took us a good half hour to round up six sheep, drop the drawbridge, and lead them into the cave. They started getting nervous as soon as they entered the cave, so we decided it was best to feed the eagle one at a time to reduce the panic it would cause the other sheep. I led the first one down into the chamber and the creature barely let out a bleat of terror before it was down the eagle's gullet. The next five went in rapid succession and the eagle looked noticeably better after the meal.

"I am Stonewall," I introduced myself while it ate the last one.

"I am Thand, giant eagle in the court of the Eagle King," he replied once the last of the sheep cleared its throat.

"Pleased to meet you, Thand. I'm going to approach you and cut your bonds, as long as you promise not to eat us." The eagle nodded and voiced his assent. I warily sidled to the back of the eagle and started cutting the roots. The plan was to make some initial cuts but position myself within range of Zew's and Hypatia's spears and Diana's flashing blades for the last cut. Our backs would be to the passage leading up for an easy retreat, just in case Thand didn't feel like keeping his end of the bargain. Unfortunately, the roots were difficult to cut and I was making excruciatingly slow progress alone—I really needed a saw to get the job properly done. After fifteen minutes of struggle, Diana and Hypatia joined in with their knives.

"So, how did this happen?" I inquired as I worked at the roots.

"Pelagos laid a trap of these roots and baited it with a fat ewe. I foolishly believed him a simpleton and fell victim to his subterfuge."

"We slew Pelagos, so he won't trap any others. He tried to trap us as well."

"Trap you? Why didn't he just slay you?" Thand didn't bother hiding his surprise; I suppose we didn't look like much of a threat to creatures that were twenty feet tall.

"We washed up on a beach a few miles from here," I explained. "We're in a metal ship which we're trying to launch back into the sea, and he was going to fill in the escape canal that we've spent days digging. I think he just wanted to keep us here so he could eat us at his leisure."

"He did enjoy his food frozen," the eagle commented. I wondered silently how long Thand had been here to know something like that—at least more than a year.

"Why did he imprison you for so long?"

But instead of answering, Thand flexed his still-mighty muscles and—snap—off came the rest of the roots. We hastily retreated to the passage as he struggled to regain his feet while spreading his enormous wings. Fighting muscle atrophy, the giant eagle took to his feet and let loose a terrifying cry of joy and liberation. This pressed us deeper into our withdrawal and he followed us upward, bending his twenty-two feet to fit into the passage.

We retreated as quickly as possible, hoping to avoid being caught underfoot in his gaining speed. The pulse of his pounding legs hounded us as Thand strove for the sky. Nearly sprinting as we cleared the cave, we joined the others huddled together with spears out against the rocky side of the entrance. The eagle burst through the hanging roots, shedding them like rivulets of water as he barreled past us with another terrifying cry. He spread his sixty-foot wings, filling the air with debris, and then he was gone.

"By Zeus, that was terrifying!" Eleutherios swore as Thand disappeared into the night.

"I've never seen anything like that before!" Phocus exclaimed, breaking his normal restraint.

We caught our collective breath before returning to the cave to explore the passage beyond Thand's prison. It was dark enough inside that I needed my flashlight and as I suspected, it led to Pelagos's treasure chamber. Who knows how long he or his ancestors had claimed this cave? The room was filled with spears, muskets, and other weaponry—all in bad condition: weathered, and worthless—but what attracted everyone were the four rusty man-sized helmets filled with silver and gold coins.

Eleutherios had the honor of counting the coins and we all squatted with her by the light of a single flashlight, watching as she laid the coins in stacks of ten, then in rows of ten, as if she were a medieval exchequer. The final tally was four hundred twenty silver ladies and six hundred thirty-six gold eagles. As the last coin was counted, Hypatia crowed "Split seven ways that's—"

"Sixty ladies and ninety eagles each," I chimed in, "with six eagles left over."

Telesilla and Hypatia burst out laughing and Phocus started crying with happiness. This much wealth meant when they finally left the isle, they not only kept their lives, but they would be rich. Not just rich, but crazy rich. Life-changingly rich.

"Before we get carried away," Eleutherios cautioned, "we should put some aside for the families of Hylas, Idas, Castor, and Butes. They'll be in need, and we should honor those of us who fell by gifting their families."

"But Periclymenus can go to hell, right?" Phocus asked with an uncharacteristic brutality in his voice.

A cruel and harsh grin spread on Eleutherios's face, "Oh, he'll go to hell all right...with a little help by the empress's justice for his desertion!"

After a discussion that went long into the night—it was dark out and we decided to sleep in the cave, regardless its pungency—we accepted that twelve eagles belonged to the each of the fallen, which reduced our take to eighty-four eagles each, but we didn't split the silver.

Chapter Twenty One

Over and Out

We were all so excited we had trouble sleeping. Today, we would try and free the *Agōgós*. The morning came slowly and cold, but finally the sun rose and we slammed down the last of the mutton along with the last of the beans. It had been a week since we'd returned from the cyclops's cave, and we'd relentlessly worked against the ever-chilling air to break out into the water before winter claimed us.

The elevation difference between the canal and the point-class cutter made this last bit of excavation too risky to work at from within the canal itself—if the ship gave, you could be crushed beneath it. We repurposed the long pointed poles we used as digging sticks to prod at the soil underneath the ship while standing on the sides. The hope was to weaken the soil so much that the shape of the ship coupled with gravity would be enough to drop the cutter into the canal, but after hours of poking and prodding, there was no appreciable effect. It was rather maddening.

We ate lunch in a foul mood, discussing alternative approaches when suddenly, the *Agōgós* lurched to the starboard, falling with a mass of dirt into the canal tunnel, propagating a man-sized wave down the length of the canal and out into the mild surf.

Once the dust settled and we realized nothing was broken, an involuntary cheer rose, noise clambering from the small group of dirty, smelly sentients desperate to leave. The *Agōgós* was stuck in the canal, bow jammed into the soil beneath the water, but at least it was facing the right way and it was in the canal! All it would take was more time to increase it. With renewed vigor, we split and attacked the canal at different locations: at the mouth to deepen the canal, along the sides to widen the canal, and near the ship, clearing as much dirt and sand in hopes the cutter would fall deep enough into the water to either float on its own or for us to slide it out manually. It was grueling, wet work, complicated by the coldness of the knee-deep water. We couldn't stay in it longer than a half hour before retreating to the revitalizing warmth of the fire.

We worked until the sun started descending and managed to open the mouth of the canal down to waist deep, but by that time, we had to start pushing the canal into the open water and we couldn't effectively move the earth into deeper water. I worried that the *Agōgós* wouldn't launch without deepening the canal further; according to my database, the draft of the point-class cutter—the vertical distance between the waterline and the bottom of the hull—was listed as just under six feet. Three to four feet of water was what we had but it was worth a try before embarking on harder, more perilous underwater excavation, but all that was academic until we got the *Agōgós* further down the canal.

We surrendered for the day and huddled around the fire, eating the last of the most-recent buck I'd bagged. All of us were looking down at our food, so we missed the two giant shadows in the pink crepuscular rays and were utterly taken aback when two giant eagles landed fifty yards to our south. Our surprise didn't last long, and our hands found our weapons within seconds. The eagles slowly walked toward us—their beaks eighteen feet off the ground—and halted thirty yards away.

"Which of you is the emancipator of Thand?" the first eagle spoke in Finnish, its voice thick and duo-toned in a consistent fifth interval.

I edged my way in front of Diana. "I am. My Finnish is poor; do you know English?"

The eagles bowed, bringing their beaks a mere foot above the ground before returning to their full height. "The mighty King of the Eagles Sorontar Landroval has dispatched us to invite you and your company to Manland Isle," the eagle replied in perfect English. "Your rescue of his son Thand requires he provide appropriate largess, even if you are only human."

I bowed. "We appreciate the king's beneficence, but are currently unable to immediately accept his offer, as our ship is stranded upon the shore and we do not know when we will be able to free it."

The eagle's head twisted side to side. "May we approach your vessel?"

I glanced to Eleutherios, who gave me a nod. "Certainly! We were washed ashore doing the great storm and are trying to build a canal back to the sea, but we have not managed to reach the depth we need," I explained as the two eagles strutted around the *Agōgós*, inspecting our work and looking back and forth amongst themselves, as if communicating.

"Do you have rope?" the other eagle asked, its voice also duo-toned but in an octave.

"Yes."

"Enough that we could hold and pull your ship free?"

I looked at Eleutherios for her expert opinion—no one knows a ship like her captain—and she nodded again. "Yes, we have enough."

"Fetch it and tie one end into a loop, and the other to the front of the ship," the first eagle commanded, "and we will drag your boat into the water."

That put the fire under the remaining crewmembers. The beach was a bustle of activity and a pair of loops appeared at the end of two one-hundred-yard-long ropes tied off at the bow. Each of the eagles grabbed one of the loops with their formidable claws and strutted to the shore where they separated and then soared into the air. By all rights, they shouldn't have been able to fly, but they took off like their regular-sized namesakes and the ropes were immediately taut. The *Agōgós* groaned as its bow was violently lifted up out of the muck.

We gathered behind it, pushing with the flat ends of our digging sticks, adding as much forward force as we could muster. All at once, the static friction broke and the cutter finally moved.

I yelled at the crew to keep applying pressure as we split down the sides of the canal, pushing the point-cutter toward the freshwater sea only yards away, straining with everything we had.

As the vessel inched out of the canal, the eagles strained under its full weight before the hull finally left the bottom in the surf and once again, the *Agōgós* bobbed freely on the waves. Relief rushed through me, and judging by the teary eyes of the remaining crew, I wasn't the only one feeling grateful for our luck.

The eagles dropped their ropes upon the deck and hovered next to us, raising a cloud of dust and spray. "Now you can come to Manland and you can overwinter to be properly gifted for your deeds," the first eagle intoned over the din of flapping wings.

"We'll be there by morning!" Eleutherios cried out as they turned, flying off into the darkness of the rapidly falling night.

We climbed into the dinghy and boarded the *Agōgós*, happy to be once again on the metal ship above its grumbly engine. Pulling out of the bay, Diana leaned over to me and asked, "What are you going to ask the king for?"

"Boredom—I could really go for a few months of boredom. Yeah, that sounds like the perfect gift."

Epilogue

The brisk wind cut through the thick woolens wrapped around me. My face was ice cold and if I was this chilled, Zew must be a Popsicle; for the second time that day, I tugged at the rope wrapped around Thand's leg and we descended to the earth. There was no need to flap during the descent and we smoothly coasted over the Southern Kingdom of Mole Men, dotted with patches of snow that lingering into early spring, before landing five minutes later. Everyone knew the drill as we had done this numerous times since we'd left Manland. Thand settled into a field next to a large woody copse and I was off gathering wood before Gelir and Hartha landed with Zew and Diana.

Once on the ground, my travel companions joined in the hunt for firewood and we built a roaring blaze within the half hour. The giant eagles closed around the fire, blocking the northern wind with their bodies as we huddled along the southern side, absorbing as much heat as we could. The eagles stayed for fifteen minutes, helping us tip over the edge from dangerously cold to normally cold, before taking to the air to hunt for the next hour. I could tell they found our incessant mammalian need for heat annoying but diplomatically said nothing about it.

King Sorontar's hospitality was fine enough, but after months of overwintering, we were all ready to go home. After a fond farewell to the crew of the *Agōgós*, who took to the water as soon as it was reasonably safe, we took to the sky toward Deeplac. This was the last task of the life debt and I think Thand was just glad to be rid of it, not just because we puny "humans"—a term the giant eagles broadly applied to any vaguely humanoid sentient that wasn't avian, regardless of actual heritage—needed frequent pit stops. Our trip was the final reminder of his long imprisonment; after this, the eagle prince would truly be free again.

Once the avian trio flew off, we took the flat rocks we'd used as heat reserves out from under our wraps and leaned them into the fire, warming them up again. The idea was an old survivalist technique, and once we'd found the right rocks, they'd served us well. Once they were hot, we'd wrap them up again and put them next to our chests for the next leg of our flight.

"How far do we have to go now?" Zew inquired with a mixture of dread and hope. Gauging by how harsh he found the cold, it didn't seem he'd spent much time in places with hard winters. After all, New Greece wasn't a cold land.

"If we go as far as we did this time, I think we'll get there in one more flight," I reassured him. We were only a few hundred miles away from Deeplac, and the giant eagles made good time. There were worse ways of traveling, even if it wasn't climate-controlled. As an added side benefit, I was able to create a detailed and current aerial map of the lands we flew over—that's got to come in handy eventually.

"If that's case, you can use my rock this trip," Diana stated matter-of-factly to Zew. "I'll help you double up and wrap it against your back." Diana had that indifference to cold that only those native to cold climes possessed; in my time, she would have been the person wearing shorts and a T-shirt when it was sunny and over 45°F. She didn't need the rocks like we did, even if she appreciated their presence. Zew gave a shivering nod of appreciation to her offer and continued huddling so close to the fire that he risked the flame. The eagles returned an hour later, traces of blood around their mouths and talons indicating a successful hunt. They again acted as wind blocks for us weak mammals, and we took to the air after another half hour of warming.

Taking off was far more exciting than landing. We'd walk off about a hundred yards and then spread out across the area. The eagles would take to the air, strongly flapping to maintain their level altitude and they'd sweep forward, grabbing us in their powerful talons as they passed. It was both thrilling and terrifying as my monkey mind simultaneously screamed "I don't want to be food!" and "Whee!" Once we were in their grip, we'd tie our safety ropes around one of their legs and then fight against the ever-growing cold as they climbed to about a thousand feet—their minimum preferred altitude to reduce the chance of stray gunfire. More than one giant eagle had taken a bullet from some land-bound idiot having a bit of fun.

We didn't have a way to communicate with Deeplac, so once I could see it through my binoculars, I had the eagles set us down—there wasn't a need to risk them being shot by one of our own. The final landing was the smoothest of them all, but that's the way of things—it seems like you achieve mastery at the moment you no longer need to perform the task.

Once we'd untied ourselves, Thand addressed us, "The debt owed to you has been repaid."

"It has," I replied. "We are thankful to you and wish you a safe return to your home."

The great eagles took a bow and the three of them lifted into the cold spring air. They banked to the northwest and accelerated to their full speed, flying higher and faster than they had while carrying us. At the rate they were going, they'd be home by tomorrow.

As we watched them fly away, Diana turned toward Deeplac. "Ready to go home?" she asked the empty air.

"More than ready!" I replied with anticipation, even though she wasn't talking to me. "I've got candy to dish out to all the kiddos."

"I could go for some haggis," Zew concurred.

"Let's get going then."

THE END

Stonewall will next appear in *Stonewall Against the Mole Men.*

www.ingramcontent.com/pod-product-compliance
Lightning Source LLC
Chambersburg PA
CBHW030222180626
46810CB00008B/2925